no good for digging

dustin m. hoffman

word west press | missoula, mt

isbn: 978-1-7334663-0-1

published by word west in missoula, mt.

first us edition 2019.
printed in the usa.

www.wordwest.co

cover & interior design: word west.

For Wendell Mayo

"Who kneels down in that church? I'll tell you who kneels. The man kneels who's settin' the toilets in the restrooms. He's got to kneel, that's part of his work. The man who nails the pews on the floor, he had to kneel down... Any work, you kneel down—it's a kind of worship. It's part of the holiness of things, work, yes. Just like drawing breath is. It's necessary. If you don't breathe, you're dead. It's kind of a sacrament, too."

  -Nick Lindsay, Carpenter/Poet, from Studs Terkel's *Working*

"To survive the day is triumph enough for the walking wounded among the great many of us."

  -Studs Terkel

Thanks to the men and women who survived building houses with me in Michigan. For those who didn't survive, these stories are especially for you.

I greatly appreciate the generous editors at Word West. Working with Julia Alvarez and Joshua Graber and David Queen has been such a pleasure. It's a rare, precious thing to have one's work honored so fully, and I will forever be grateful.

Thanks to the fine editors who first published these stories in their magazines: "A Nesting" in *Wigleaf*, "Red Shoe Twitch" in *Yalobusha Review*, "The Magician's Secret" in *Juked*, "An All-Night Diner" in *Naugatuck River Review*, "A Realistic Airplane" in *The Saturday Evening Post*, "Grandpa Dies" in *Quarterly West*, "Moon Burn" in *Other Poetry*, "My Pupils, Dive Sites" and "Long Division" in *Gargoyle*, "Father's Knots" in *Columbia Journal*, "The Plumber who Found Treasure" in *Hobart*, "A Better Trap" and "The Mouth Full of Flying" in *Barely South*, "On the Strongest Man Compound" in *Parcel*, "Hair Cropper Shies" and "The Life Model" in *Word Riot*, "Postal Heterochromia" and "Interstate Intestine" in *New South*, "The Ouija Board Inspector" in *The Forge Literary Magazine*, "Pitch" in *Pleiades*, "To Wait for Landing" and "Angel in the Pit" in *Crannóg*, "The Diviner" in *Grasslimb*, "When We" in *Necessary Fiction*, "The Life Net" in *Moon City Review*, "Amateur Paleontologist Stumbles into My Foot" in *Monkeybicycle*, "Father at Shift End" in *Bateau*, "Brandy's Streetlamp" in *REAL: Regarding Arts and Letters*, "No Good for Digging," in *Green Mountains Review*, "Bruise Room" in *Cold Mountain Review*.

I'm so grateful for the friendship and support of my colleagues at Winthrop University, especially Siobhan Brownson, Ephraim Scott Sommers, Casey Cothran, Matthew Fike, and Gregg Hecimovich. Thanks to Ronald Parks for composing stunning music with my art. Thanks to Tom Stanley for inspiring "Father at Shift End" with his series of paintings called *The Neighborhood*. Thanks to Téa Franco for her editorial work. I owe so much to my amazing Winthrop students, who challenge me to be better, to try and keep up with their brilliance.

So many amazing writers helped me get these stories right. Their wisdom and generosity have freed me from countless horrific drafts. Thanks Joseph Celizic, Brad Aaron Modlin, Anne Valente, Brandon Davis Jennings, Glenn Deutsch, David Williams, Jacqueline Vogtman, Bridget Dooley, Dan Mancilla, Matt Bell, and Jef Otte. I owe endless gratitude to my teachers who encouraged me to follow stories down whatever strange hole I was digging. Thanks to Lawrence Coates, Sharona Muir, Thisbe Nissen, Nancy Eimers, Theresa Williams, Jon Adams, Adam Schuitema, Jaimy Gordon, and the great Wendell Mayo. I hope to honor Wendell with every sentence I write.

Thanks to Mom and Dad, sisters Heather and Holly, for endless support. Finally, none of this would ever be possible or matter nearly as much without my partner Carrie, and my two favorite little humans Evelyn and Alison.

CONTENTS

A NESTING

A nest of birds complained behind the sheetrock. We could hear their beaks clacking studs, their baby wings fluttering in tangles of pink fiberglass insulation. As we worked on installing cabinets and tacking carpet and touching up paint, they shrieked. This new home would be forever haunted by hollow bones and black feathers.

We blamed the drywallers and they blamed the framers and they blamed the landscapers. But we all carried hammers. They hung at our hips, nestled in our truck beds, rested like the dead in toolbox caskets. Any one of us could have punched a hole and turned finished walls to fluttering.

RED SHOE TWITCH

Barry buried me in the Escape Cube, six feet down. Though it's not a cube. It's a plexiglass casket, more of a rectangle. I built it. Barry named it. He convinced me to test it, but now it's been too long since I stopped hearing dirt shush against the plexiglass top. Maybe he's still pissed about the time I misplaced the key and after a half-hour of writhing we had to knife him out of the straight jacket in front of the San Bernardino Lion's club and all their booing grandkids. I said I was sorry. I didn't complain when he docked the jacket's price from my pay. Now I'm thinking bygones aren't all gone.

My phone reports its twenty-percent battery life left, and maybe I should turn the light off. But everything inside the Escape Cube seems louder in the dark—my breath, my skin squeaking against the plexiglass, the whispering dirt grains piling at my ankle. I suppose I'll keep the light on until it dies.

Staring into a plexiglass wall of dirt, I confront the fact that I'm in my forties, earning an income subsisting of whatever scraps Barry feels like paying me. I can't even get the under-the-table construction jobs anymore, and they sure as shit won't let me build anymore stunt props on the studios since the accident. You know the one. Everyone remembers her name, Florence Hudson. It was her on-set tragedy. But, thank Christ, no one remembers my name. Video went viral—Florence's shiny red shoe twitching for too many seconds under all those sheets of collapsed OSB. Barry embraces death. Mortal inevitability, he told me when he hired me two years ago, infuses the show with a necessary pulse.

Should I have crammed myself inside this box? Barry is certainly aware of my claustrophobia. Joke's on him. After thirty-three minutes down here, I'm feeling much better about small spaces. I'm sold on exposure therapy. I glance down at my bare toes, my twitching feet. I think of the trapped kid's shiny red shoe and rehearse the regret of how I should've used twice as many deck screws, should've stood up to that goddamn director rushing me, should've shown my face at Florence's funeral, and then I'd know if she was here now, just as deep and only a few plots separating us. Next comes pondering plexiglass joint strength, that acrylic cement clear as water against however many tons of earth, against so much weight stacked over my face. I'm aching to stretch my limbs. So maybe traces of my claustrophobia linger.

Probably I deserve this. I told him an escape-from-the-grave act didn't seem best for an elementary school. What about rabbits in hats and bright bouquets erupting from thin air, I'd said. I could hack together a flashy trap-door box for a disappearing act, I'd offered. He clapped a hand against my cheek, pulled my forehead against his, and said so slowly I thought I'd melt: We are not magicians. We are escapists.

Yeah, Barry. Of course, Barry. My bad, Barry. But I would like to point out that I am not an escapist. I'm strictly props. I'm the hammer and nails, the measuring tape and drill bit behind the curtain. I'm the saw.

But this all might be about Kate. Miserable Kate who I didn't even fuck. It never got anywhere near that far, and it's not like they're married anyway. A ring, a promise, stretched over five years—just until we land that fat Las Vegas contract, baby—does not a commitment make. Yet still I refrained. Kate snotted all over my car about how Barry doesn't trust her, still hasn't introduced her to his dying grandmother Poleski, about how Barry only goes down on her for thirty seconds, exactly thirty, every time, and then makes a joke about how Houdini could hold his breath for four minutes but he was the master. Worst of all, she uttered through tears, is that Barry won't even tell her the secret to how he escapes from the grave.

4

Me too, Kate. Me too.

I've already kicked and punched my hands raw, but—what the hell, I'll take up another round of flailing. I've also already screamed my throat raw as gravel, coppery with blood, so this time I just howl, high pitched, as long as I can hold the note, which times out shorter than Houdini could hold his breath and about as long as Barry's cunnilingus.

The trickling dirt has completely buried my feet now. That's on me. Bad seal somewhere. I'll probably die in here, suffocate or be crushed like the kid and her twitching red shoe. I thumb a few texts to my mom, my favorite English teacher, my sisters, all about the same: *Thanks for the good times. Guess you were right about Barry. I never thought I'd hurt anyone. If you find my body, please don't bury me again. Set it all on fire.*

My ears ring from the howling, or maybe they're not ringing. Maybe it's some kind of subterranean echo. Maybe the worms have taken up my hymn. Maybe Florence is siren-singing me to join her. I clamp my lips and hold my breath to test the sound's reality. It rings. It sings, begging me. It rises and falls. Metallic. Beautiful as a shovel exhuming earth, as my salvation. Florence and her shoe won't stop twitching if you just keep replaying the video and never let it end.

THE MAGICIAN'S SECRET

How many were killed for the magician's secret?

149,366 humans have murdered each other thus far for the magician's secret. However, the number rises every day.

How is the secret kept?

262,144 sentinels guard the magician's secret, scribed upon a leathered elephant ear, inked with bioluminescent squid blood. The magician's neck was then slit by a guard who stowed the secret in an adamantine box and delivered it to a mountain. This guard and his lover protect the box. Four more guards—all lovers—locked the couple inside a larger titanium vault, which they guard. Eight guards guard a larger steel vault. Sixteen an iron vault. Thirty-two—yes, all deeply in love with one another—guard a bamboo cage. Sixty-four the mouth of the cave gated in elephant femur. 128 interlock arms to create a body wall that blocks the mountain path. And this builds onward until we reach the 131,072 love-sick soldiers who circle the shores surrounding the island housing the mountain wherein resides a cave mouth that swallowed so many lovers and one secret.

How long have they guarded?

No one has checked on the original guard pair. We assume they are dead. But, rest assured, their exponential brethren provide adequate security, depending on how many of them have not died of dehydration, starvation, loneliness.

What is the secret?
We can't be tricked.

Who was the magician?
He harbored an affinity for tangerines. He was lactose intolerant and suffered from irritable bowel syndrome and mild methemoglobinemia that tinted his skin sky blue. He loved his mother, grew bored of his father's shouting. He always wanted a pet tortoise, but never found a way to work one into his act.

What was his name?
No one remembers. So much we have documented and filed, and yet his name remains an omission. Most suspect there was a J involved. Historians have proposed theories of a "son" in the surname. Linguists have argued over a sacred schwa or a holy diphthong. Philosophers demand that his name never existed, is mere distraction. Only the secret matters.

What is the secret?
No one can ever know.

Are there other secrets?
None as important.

Why this secret?
Despite all we've forgotten, we all can recite the Day of Witness. All who witnessed, which was nearly everyone after the video impregnated every screen, raved madly. There was pure joy, yes, at the miracle, and some of us wept for days, kneeling at the spot where we watched, in theatre aisles, on our home couches or toilets, inside our cars waiting at red lights. Others, however, most of us, the weakest of us, couldn't handle the majesty and stuffed our ears with grass, sealed our eyes with epoxy, stitched our lips tight with needle and thread. We couldn't imagine lives spent witnessing any miracle of lesser wonder. The world's population fractioned into one-tenth within three days. And on that first Day of Witness, not a soul moved.

Yet you don't remember?

We remember the magician's tuxedo, how it appeared rented, cheap, a yellowish ghost of a stain on his chest. We remember his face seeming childlike, how it made us want to hug our children in sympathy with his inevitable embarrassment. We remember his assistant's white feather boa, her green sequins, her white teeth and the black hole of her missing incisor. The magic trick itself involved, maybe: a horse, a wooden box, a saw, two doves, the Empire State building, the assistant's lower torso, the Hope Diamond, a deck of cards with all the kings removed, three reticulated pythons, one white rabbit, a ten-thousand-gallon tank of sea water containing seventeen poisonous jellyfish and one mako shark, a pair of handcuffs, a red silk kerchief, and countless doors that may have been trapped, but we dare not guess.

What is the secret?

How can anyone know?

Is it the principle?

We are not magicians. We are not bound by any oath. We do not, like the Free Masons, like the International Brotherhood of Magicians, chum around in wood-paneled lodges chanting before sacred, leather-bound texts. We are guided only by the need to protect our children's children from obsession.

What is the secret?

We do, however, understand endless asking. We who have witnessed have patience and compassion and bountiful tolerance.

At least, then, what color is the secret?

You would think yellow, like the magician's stained shirt. Or black like his jacket and the assistant's missing tooth. But, no, it is beige. Sandy in texture. A fine sand, not like the coarse bone grinds of the magician's cremated remains, but like the desert.

And its smell?
We've already said too much.

What value does the secret hold? In American dollars? In Euros? In rupees? In yen? Does it depreciate? Does it stand up to inflation?
No war was ever fought over a prize with no value. For proof of value, inspect the death toll, which has not slowed, despite inflation. However, our economists really can't calculate an exact number when they're unsure about the status of those inner guards and their lovers.

When will the secret be revealed?
There is a time set in place. There is a time and a place. But concerning that day and hour, no one knows. Not even the guards. Not even their lovers.

If the secret could be a stone or smoke, which would it be?
Stone.

Does it glow with radiation?
Of course.

If you could compare it to any intergalactic heavenly body...
Ask what you truly mean to ask.

What is the secret?
Ask a better question.

How much does it hurt to be sawed?
The assistant's diary reveals that on their twentieth anniversary of marriage and assistantship, she asked that her only gift be to know. He refused. Two nights later, at their next performance, he sawed as he always had. But this time, for the first time, she felt the steel teeth gnaw into her skin, her ribs, her lungs. The crowd watched her blood cascade in sheets atop the white-marble stage floor. She witnessed herself spilling. But then he huzzah-ed the crowd, flipped the box

open, and the assistant found her body uncut, untouched, wholly there. He grabbed her hands and swooped her into a kiss, and his mouth, she reports, tasted of blood.

What is the name of the first guard's lover?
His name is or was Salazar. Warring soldiers wear his name tattooed on their left breast. This faction fights for freedom of the guards, past and present, and care nothing about the secret. They've chosen freedom over knowledge. We pity them. We envy them. Our left breasts remain unmarked.

And what about the first guard?
His lover's memory surpasses him. The slitter of magician throats is lost to history. Though some of us might have his oath tattooed in the webbing of our toes, script so small you'd need a magnifying glass to discern the words written in a dead language that only three scholars in the world can translate.

What is the secret?
It's been so long.

What is the secret?
The experts have all died. The guards who remember what they're guarding are all dead. Generations dedicated to forgetting what they knew and what their fathers knew have succeeded and then faded away to dust.

What is the secret?
Perhaps there never was one.

What of all the blood?
Yes, there is always the blood.

What is the secret?
It stretches in seafoam-green tentacles across the night sky.

What is the secret?

A boy once knew. A boy once loved a guard who died knowing what could never be known.

What is the secret?

Only the dead know. Do you truly want to witness?

We are asking.

Despite all the blood?

And buckets more.

Then this will never end.

AN ALL-NIGHT DINER

is open inside my heart, left atrium. Late, an elderly couple gaze at one another from across the bar. They don't speak, don't need to—they follow routine, downing full coffee mugs and dropping them in tandem—*slurp, thud, crack, slurp, thud, crack*. Regulars. They never leave. Never tip well.

My heart is downtown, a college town. Drunken students file in, suffering 3:00 AM hunger for eggs and corned beef hash, which many of them will vomit in my stalls. Some don't make it and vomit in the aisle. My heart heaves with excitement, until student eyes become heavy like bowling balls. They file out, back to the liver. We wish them well, pray they don't crash into anything important—so thin the capillary two-tracks, the tight-shouldered arteries. How we love the students, those minutes of irregularity.

Now the elderly couple is fighting quietly, eying the last creamer. We all worry about the drunks, but let's not act like children. The creamer truck will come tomorrow, new students will starve and spew next week, and you two are welcome to stay, but please lift your feet as I sweep, and, please, stop leaving pennies for the waitress.

A REALISTIC AIRPLANE

Felix drew a P-66 Vanguard fighter plane, an old one, a beauty, just like the one he'd seen in the book at school called *Wings of War*, on the back of a yellow envelope marked "Final Notification." He sketched the cockpit while his grandma wheezed on the other end of the phone. It was the first aviation drawing he'd created in his nine years of life where he'd gotten the angle right so that the wings didn't look like disproportional stubs. He felt the chill of brilliance sneaking through his fingers and up into his throat. He would have told his grandma he was nearing mastery, if the phone speaker hadn't been so full of gasp, choke, and then thunk.

Felix dotted a few last rivets on the airplane's shell. He handed the phone to his dad when his grandma stopped talking. He wasn't sure she was dead, but he had an idea, a picture in his mind— charred bodies strewn in ditches in black-and-white photos, like the photographs in the book at school called *Victory at Great Expense*. He decided he might draw a corpse someday, since the airplane had turned out so well. He pushed the envelope on which he'd drawn the plane toward his dad, who was shouting into the receiver. His dad slammed down the phone, picked it back up, and punched the numbers 9-1-1. Felix knew those numbers were for emergencies only. He'd learned that in a booklet at school featuring a husky dog wearing a beret that remonstratively shook his paw at a pack of snickering wolves. The booklet was called *Crying Wolf and Real Emergencies*. Felix avoided dialing numbers as much as possible for this very reason. He feared his fingers might slip and accidentally dial 9-1-1 and then he'd go to jail and never own a husky.

His dad shouted into the phone. His fingers tightened around the envelope featuring Felix's excellently drawn airplane, crinkling the nose and whirring propeller. His dad didn't look at it, but when he finally did, Felix knew he'd be impressed, would forget all about Mrs. Murdock's Social Butterflies Bar Graph that had shown up in the mailbox last week along with a batch of red and yellow envelopes stamped "Notice." On the graph, all the kids in Felix's class were represented by pastel rectangles. But Felix was crimson. He didn't like the color that was like the envelopes his dad swore at and were too dark to draw on. He didn't like that his rectangle was the stubbiest. He wasn't stupid because he could read everything and he remembered everything and he finished his Mad Minute Math problems either first or second after Wilson Betts. And he didn't like the way Mrs. Murdock described him: *Felix keeps to himself, sometimes hides his head in his flip-top desk, where he stashes half-eaten tuna sandwiches. The other kids hold their noses and call him Fishy Felix.* His dad had pulled the note away before he could read the rest. But he'd only hid his head in his flip-top desk four times. And he hid tuna sandwiches because he might get hungry between lunch and the end of school. It was a matter of saving, like his dad said. When you have enough saved, nothing can hurt you.

They'd beat the ambulance to Grandma's, Felix's dad bet. Felix was already wearing his coat because it was October and his dad saved by keeping the heat off. The TV screen turned to snow and fizz last month, and last week the lights stopped, even his night light shaped like a princess. He hated that princess, wished she was a P-66 bomber, but he missed her pink light. Maybe the princess looked like his mom. Maybe his mom was nothing like that. He'd grown out of imagining his mom as a princess or astronaut or professional wrestler. Grown out of that like his dad had grown out of his job at Burger King. His dad could do better than a hairnet and minimum wage and he had to. Felix agreed completely with the concept of unrecognized potential. Felix would fix airplanes, like his dad who fixed cars, who'd fixed their Cutlass's shot starter three days ago. Without his skill, the car wouldn't have started up so beautifully, his dad said, so that they could rush to Grandma's house and help. Helping family was most important.

"I love your grandma, Felix. You can tell by the way I'm crying. See." His dad took a hand from the steering wheel, wiped his cheek, and brushed a wet warmth against Felix's hand. "It's okay for a guy to cry sometimes. Remember how to be sad. Whatever happens with Grandma is okay. It's okay to feel any way you want."

Felix dried his wet hand inside his pocket. He wanted to tell his dad how he'd figured out that crying didn't fix anything. That might make his dad feel better to know it didn't help to feel bad. But he also knew how much he hated when teachers told him how he should feel. So Felix concentrated, closed his eyes and traced lines against his eyelids. The corpse drawing was shaping perfectly in his mind. He just needed some blank paper to draw on.

GRANDPA DIES

The first time Grandpa died we were at the circus. Trapeze artists swung from pencil-thin bars, and I waited for one to fall. At nine years old, I questioned the strength of safety netting, imagined one frayed thread. A puddle of blood would bloom from sequined leotard and glitter hairspray.

Grandpa whistled to himself each time one of them somersaulted through the air. He lowered his mouth so close to my ear I could hear the saliva bubbles on his fat lips. He whispered, "One in five circus acrobats end their careers with a mashed noggin." Then he leaned back in his seat. "If anyone dies, I hope it's not the one with the impressive hooters," he said.

I wanted to shush him, but we were in the back row. It was the last day before the tent folded up and left town, and only a dozen or so bodies spotted the hundreds of empty seats. I focused on the impressive hooters, asked God to watch over them. I squeezed my snow cone until blue syrup oozed cold and sticky onto my knuckles. Grandpa asked if I wanted another snow cone, and I said nothing as the artists swung higher, closer and closer to the tent's peak. Grandpa offered to buy me cotton candy, a pennant, a pink balloon shaped like an elephant. The men clutched the women's ankles, released them, catapulting their shiny torsos into triple spins.

Grandpa slid his arm over my shoulder and pointed up. I followed his hairy arm, that thick index finger slashed by the white scar he told me he got when a hungry table saw

19

tried to eat him for lunch. "The real magic is right there in the rigging," Grandpa said. "Ten tons of canvas, pulleys and straps, frame poles thicker than elephant bones. The invisible hero of the circus is the tent man, who whips a palace together in a few hours. That's the wonder here."

I tried to think of men propping up striped canvas, but my eyes strayed from Grandpa's finger. The leotard princess stood on a tiny pedestal, bent at the waist, fingers spread in the spotlight as the bar floated into her palms.

Grandpa gasped, squeezed my shoulder so hard I thought it would pop. Then his grip went loose. His body crumpled like a fallen acrobat.

I prodded his belly, pinched his sandpaper cheek. He didn't move. My snow cone splashed onto my sneakers. I slipped my finger under his nose. No breath. I straddled his limp body, shook his shoulders, missed the princess swinging back up to the platform unscathed.

No one in the scattered audience glanced my way when Grandpa died, when the tears ran down my cheeks. Because of those sparkling trapeze artists, no one cared. We were invisible as those tent men. So I screamed. I like to imagine the glimmering leotards all paused, their sequins gleaming a hundred tiny spotlights my way, contorted bodies frozen in midair. But I didn't get to see it. I was facing my dead grandpa, whose right arm woke from death and clapped over my mouth.

"Someone dies of a heart attack every thirty-three seconds," he whispered. "It'll happen when you least expect, so never forget to keep one eye on the world and the other on Grandpa."

I missed the trapeze artists' four-person swinging chain, their famous denouement. I was busy counting seconds. Every time I hit thirty-three-Mississippi, someone died somewhere, and I squinted at Grandpa to confirm his living.

Really the first time Grandpa died was before I could remember anything, at the moment of my birth. In the delivery room, Grandpa manned the camcorder. I came into this world purple and silent, umbilical cord noosed around my neck.

But none of this is on film. Grandpa dropped the camcorder just as the crown of my scalp bubbled between my mother's legs. After that, the video plummets. Blue-bootied feet fill the screen, layers of yelling. My mother's groans drown in my father's shriek, the nurses' shouts. Someone kicks the camcorder and it spins to Grandpa's face, a close-up of his lolling tongue, the milky scar like a comet above his right eye pressed to the white-tiled floor. He got that scar, he once told me, serving his country, building Ike Eisenhower's interstates, a run-in with a rogue jackhammer. Saved the foreman's life and still finished his stretch of concrete before going to the emergency room.

Did he receive the Purple Heart he deserved? No. And my parents didn't name me after him, despite how he pestered them when the hospital admitted him and gave him the bed next to my mother. My mother told me she refused him one hundred times, but Grandpa's constant chatter enveloped her thoughts. Resistance took everything she had. When my mother was ready to leave, they told my parents they had to choose. Instead of Grandpa's name, my birth certificate has "Placeholder" typed above the inky stamps of my tiny feet. They always told me they'd change it, but never did, and then when the responsibility became mine, something always seemed more important.

The only copy of the video of my birth hides on a shelf next to the other home movies. It has no label, because how do I title that? No one has ever watched it but me. And when I do, I press pause just before the film cuts out. A slit of Grandpa's pale blue iris shows through a clinched eyelid. A tenth of a second wink to a life unseen.

Grandpa died on a Tuesday once. He was demoing my parents' roof, had been at it all day, chucking broken shingles all over the yard until it looked like the earth had opened up gaping black holes. My dad kicked shingles on his way to the mattress that leaned against the big oak tree in our front yard, where he'd teach me to throw the knuckleball. He dug his fingernails into the red stitches, pinky contorted, his hand

21

like a crippled claw. It would give me the edge, I was sure, make a mediocre high school pitcher throw no-nos, get scouted, drafted, become a superstar and make millions. The whole world would watch a man who'd mastered the dying art of the knuckleball. Right as he tucked up a knee to wheel into his delivery, Grandpa shouted from the roof, "Either this roof goes or I do."

My dad shook his head and refocused on the mattress—that tiny mess of springs and stuffing I grew out of years ago. He homed in on the faded urine stains from when I was six and still wet the bed. Dad would always scrub the mattress secretly on Saturdays, never said anything about it to me or Mom or Grandpa, like it never happened.

Dad wound up, kicked his leg. A shingle spun off the roof and flew past him like a runner sprinting off his lead. Dad's neck jerked. He released. His knuckler zagged wildly, bounced into the street. I ran after it, left him smacking his glove, his back turned to Grandpa and the roof.

Dad had wanted to hire the roof out, because we didn't need to risk dancing across the steep pitch. But Grandpa said that was the problem with number men, pencil-pushers, desk jockeys. Would pay a small fortune to hide their fear of climbing ladder rungs. Dad worked as an accountant. Grandpa built his own house, worked construction for thirty years. He said he was a journeyman electrician, the finest carpenter in Cheboygan County, fastest shingler in northern Michigan. He'd consulted on plans for the Mackinac Bridge, been personally requested by the governor to oversee underwater welding after Frank Pepper ascended too quickly and died of the bends. If Grandpa's story was true, it still didn't make him famous, didn't even earn him a footnote in Michigan history books. I checked, spent all of fifth grade scouring the library. The way my dad put it, Grandpa was just an old handyman. Thirty years of labor got him nothing but a bad back, a half-dozen scars, a crooked thumb, and a right knee that popped like crazy when the sky went gray.

Out in the street, I could see Grandpa over the eave, leaning to slap his husky named Sal on the ribs. He'd carried Sal up the ladder with one arm early that morning. Sal panted now, looked like he was laughing, his hind legs straddling the peak. Sal's muzzle followed Grandpa as he scraped his rusty pitchfork against the last of the shingles. He worked quickly, his short, thick arms grinding prongs against plywood. Somehow he seemed to sense the edge of the roof without needing to look, his boots inches from stumbling into the gutter.

"You wanna kill yourself?" Dad yelled. Grandpa straightened his back, puffed out his chest, smiled. Then his smile flattened when he saw that Dad was talking to me. He aimed his pitchfork my way, slowly. The sun at his back lit his bald scalp and cast his eyes into dark shadows. Grandpa looked like a Greek god escaped from the underworld, now reigning over our torn-bare roof.

"Get out of the damn road," Dad said.

Grandpa dropped the pitchfork on the roof and scuffled closer to the roof edge. I couldn't stop watching, forgot all about the lost baseball and being drafted and standing in the road. Dad's leather mitt slapped against the sod. He jogged out to me. His lips curled to reveal grinding teeth that gleamed in the sun. He hopped the curb and swatted me on the back of the head.

Behind my dad's back, the pine shrubs shuddered, followed by a thud. Dad left me at the curb and bolted toward the house. I couldn't keep up with him, a middle-aged accountant, and that's when I knew I'd never be drafted, never tip my hat to the roar of thirty thousand fans.

He made it to the shrubs before I even got in sight of them. He yelled to me, "Everything will be all right. Don't touch your grandfather." Dad's face blurred past, but I saw enough, saw the vein popping like a fat worm on his forehead, all that white in his eyes. The front storm door gasped open, slammed shut, and then I was alone.

I crept to the house, stepping on broken shingles that crunched like snapping bones. Sal barked from the roof, lunged forward only to balk at the edge.

Grandpa's body was twisted in the shrubs, his arms splayed like a broken G.I. Joe. His eyes were closed. Dad said I shouldn't touch him, but I had to know how cold he was, find out where the bleeding came from so I could rig a tourniquet out of my T-shirt and twigs like Grandpa had taught me. I touched his forehead first, like my mom always did when I was faking sick. His forehead was warm, maybe hot, but I didn't know. I'd never touched a dead man. When I drew my hand back, Grandpa's blue eyes stared up at me. He smiled and lifted a tar-grimed finger to his lips.

I stayed quiet until the ambulance arrived, let tears stream down my dad's cheeks. I wanted to tell him, but Dad would be mad instead of leaning over Grandpa and telling him how much he loved him. To evoke those words was an art more secret than to throw a knuckleball.

The paramedics tried to lift Grandpa onto a gurney, but he pushed them away, was up and walking with the paramedics' blood pressure band still strapped around his bicep. They urged him to at least take a ride to the hospital to check for internal bleeding. He didn't need to go, he said. He felt better than ever. They shook their heads, chuckled when Grandpa whipped out the tire pressure gauge he always kept in his pocket and told them the ambulance's right rear tire was a bit low.

"Ever see a man so old walk away from a fall like this?" Grandpa asked the paramedics. He handed them beers from his cooler, which they reached for, but then waved away.

They assured him they hadn't.

"Must be some sort of record of age and distance fallen." Grandpa slapped my dad's back, said, "You should run some numbers on that."

The next day, he finished shingling the roof with Sal, said the two of them made record time, wondered if someone shouldn't call the *Cheboygan Daily*: Retired Roofer Keeps On Ticking. Dad forgot about teaching me the knuckleball. He spent the day pacing the length of the house, peering up at Grandpa, but wouldn't dare step on the first ladder rung.

Grandpa died in his bathroom when I was eleven, slipped on the tiles when I ran into his house to collect him for Christmas morning. Grandpa died when we were making a giant diorama

24

of the solar system for my eighth-grade science fair and he fell on the table saw. Grandpa burned in campfires, had aneurisms at football games when I waved to the bleachers, choked on turkey bones and once a pecan pie at Thanksgiving. Instead of studying for tests, I learned the Heimlich, mouth-to-mouth resuscitation, drew schematics for defibrillators salvaged from toaster ovens.

Grandpa didn't die on the Sunday in February when I was eighteen, when we buried Sal. Sal spent the previous night at the emergency vet hospital. I'd driven them there, picked him up an hour before midnight. I had to pull myself away from Wendy Seitzer's soft lips when Grandpa called. She'd slipped off that threadbare Relay for Life T-shirt in the front seat of my Cutlass, and her white bra glowed brighter than anything I'd ever seen at night. I scraped that T-shirt off my floormats and drove her home, my skin hot, fingers twitching. That whole drive I wanted to pull over into every empty parking lot and forget about Grandpa.

But Sal wouldn't get up, Grandpa said, wouldn't even raise his head when Grandpa waved a raw steak in front of his nose. He wouldn't get up all night at the hospital, his rib cage shuddering full, then collapsing flat. The doctor said he was old, that it was his time. Grandpa turned down the needle and the soft sleep. He cupped Sal's chin, said Sal was a tough dog, no fucking quitter.

Sal died anyway, at home on Grandpa's lap, three filet mignons piled in front of his nose. We buried him the next day, or at least we tried. The ground was frozen solid. Dad and I were in charge of digging. We snapped two shovel spades off their wooden poles and only managed a six-inch divot in the earth. Grandpa came out carrying Sal wrapped in an American flag. When he saw our hole, he was disgusted, said that shallow depth was an insult to a true patriot. Grandpa had told me about how Sal once saved the governor by biting a man at the Memorial Day parade. Sal chased that man for two miles, a train of police cruisers tailing his pursuit. Everyone thought Sal was rabid until the assassin collapsed from exhaustion and rifle casings jingled out of his breast pocket, at which point Sal lifted his leg over the crumpled body and pissed upon his face.

Grandpa told me that story when I was a child. I told all my friends at school, and only stopped when a teacher wrote a note to my parents for telling lies. But there was Sal's paw jutting out of his American flag shroud. Made up or not, Sal's heroism of thwarting crime would always dwarf our own triumphs.

Grandpa spent the rest of daylight digging. He repaired and broke the shovels a half-dozen times before he took up a splitting wedge and a sledge to chisel out another two feet of frozen dirt. It was night before Grandpa placed Sal into a respectable hole. I watched from the kitchen window that looked upon the back yard, and I wondered if I should join them, tell a true story of something I remembered about Sal.

We hadn't been invited to hear Sal's eulogy, so I sat inside imagining my floormats filled with Wendey Seitzer's crumpled clothes, imagining a world where Grandpa died years ago and I spent all night pressing my lips against Wendy's body.

Grandpa eventually slunk in through the back door and stood at the window, a statue staring all night into the darkness.

My mom's mom, Clarice, died when I was twenty. She appointed me as a pallbearer. I was afraid to do it. I didn't know how heavy a casket could be, and Clarice's looked colossal, marble finish, brass handles.

I kept visiting the casket, and Mom teared up each time I stood over Clarice's body. "My sensitive baby," Mom said, wrapping her hand around my fingers. After she released me, I gripped the casket's brass handles. I lifted as much as I dared without Mom noticing my flexing shoulders, mistaking muscle strain for mourning. But I couldn't budge it. Not even enough to rustle Clarice's freshly permed and dyed red hair.

Grandpa showed up to the viewing for the last half-hour. My mom grunted as he staggered down the aisle. "What the hell is he doing here?" She stood from her seat in the front row, crumpling the funeral program into her fist, but I intervened to meet Grandpa at the casket. His breath smelled like whisky when he pulled my forehead against his and said, "Do you think someone can die over a broken heart?"

He gripped the handles and cried. The casket shook with

his sobs, rattling on its stand so loud that everyone looked. The weight was nothing for him, a man three times my age, who'd lifted sledges and shingle stacks his whole life. I hadn't lifted more than a textbook since I'd started college. They were heavy textbooks, though. I was majoring in mechanical engineering. I wanted to become a famous inventor. Perhaps I'd create hydraulic shirt sleeves to exponentially increase arm strength—or maybe hover caskets. Of course, I'd never actually invent anything noticeable. I design rebar for a construction materials company. Millions more caskets will be dropped into the earth with no help from me.

Grandpa shuffled toward the coffee parlor in the back of the funeral home, dabbing his eyes with a paisley handkerchief he pulled from the chest pocket of his black T-shirt tucked into black jeans. Everyone in the lobby turned to watch his blubbering exit, patted him on the shoulders as he passed. Only Mom and Dad and I knew he'd only met Clarice five times over the years at Christmas dinners. We stopped inviting him after he called Clarice a goddamn liar when she said she'd served President Ford a cup of coffee with two creams at the diner she worked at when she was sixteen. Grandpa smacked the serving spoon into the mashed potatoes, shouted that Ford took his coffee black.

Mom clutched Dad's lapels and told him if he didn't deal with his child-of-a-father she'd shove her heels up Grandpa's ass. Dad looked at me, lifted his eyebrows toward the coffee parlor. As if I knew what to do about Grandpa.

I made my way to the back, dodging dozens of hands reaching to pat my blazer. The parlor was empty. A full pot of coffee simmered on the hot plate. A box of pink-frosted pastries sat heavy on a silver dish. My stomach growled, but eating a bright pastry seemed like it would be disrespectful to Clarice. I heard whimpering from behind a plum curtain. I lifted the curtain and stepped into a room filled with caskets. A dim sconce lit a massive wooden crucifix on the wall, but otherwise the room was shadows. Grandpa's whimpers continued without sign of body. Some of the caskets were open and empty, some sealed tight.

Hidden in the darkness, Grandpa blew his nose wetly.

There were no other doorways, no escape from the room. I dragged my finger across a shiny ebony casket, lifted the lid slowly, half-expecting to find another permed mop like Clarice's or a bald scalp combed over with thin gray strands, but inside was only satin. Grandpa whimpered again, like Sal used to do from behind the sofa during thunderstorms. I moved to a pink casket, and as soon as I'd cracked the lid I realized it was child-sized. Grandpa could never mash his stocky frame into the space made for a little girl. And I wondered if little girls could really die, somehow couldn't believe it. Death seemed owned by Grandpa.

Grandpa's whimper turned into what could've been a stifled chuckle, and I knew he was there, inside the lacquered oak casket engraved with a scene of an old trout fisherman, knee-deep in a stream, a young boy at his side smiling up at him. I ran my fingers over the ridges of the immaculate woodwork. After this casket left the showroom and got dumped into the ground, there'd just be worms and dirt pressing into the grooves of this idealized scene shared between grandfather and grandson.

Grandpa awaited inside that one, but I wouldn't open it. Clarice's arms were crossed and dead in her casket, but I knew he was jamming his hands over his mouth, choking back the giggles of about-to-be-found. I knew the feeling from playing hide and seek with him as a kid. I'd hide between the overalls in his closet, inhaling the scents of sawdust and turpentine, biting the pencils he left in his pockets. He always knew where to find me, and that's why I chose the spot. I was afraid to hide anywhere else, because what if he didn't find me? I couldn't waste my life waiting for someone to notice I was gone.

MOON BURN

Home from hunting, he basks in moonlight outside his silver trailer, mustachioed, lunar lip half-eclipsed. On the dark side of his face, his cheeks are craters—buckshot, a gift from his twelve-year-old-brother's 12-gauge to his face. It should have been the squirrel behind him, whose flesh they wouldn't eat, whose skin they wouldn't tan and turn into tobacco pouches under dawn's tissue-paper moon. Now he can't feel a thing except with finger-tips, and his brother has been dead for years.

Last week, the dentist found another shard of shot. He tapped a toothbrush at x-ray specks, buckshot brilliance. Inside his face—that ghost with bright white teeth—a star nested under his right cheekbone. Skull wisps and jaw fog and white star. These things can take time to surface, some slower than others, the dentist said. Next year, who knows what we'll find.

He fingers the craters, one newly scarred, still soft from extraction, his brother still no less dead. Hunting accident or suicide. How could he know? Their blinds hid on different neighboring acres. They'd split seasons since kids, since the buckshot, since the last words his brother said to him: *How bad does it hurt?* For his brother, the bullet passed right through, exit wound, clean escape, no metal glints in his skull. Now he has all season to hunt. Now he is the lone astronaut imagining a star inside.

29

MY PUPILS, DIVE SITES

each for a speleologist. The first scruffs her black hair, short like a boy's. The other snaps her bleached ponytail between rubber-skinned wetsuit and tan flesh. They wade my tear marshes, check gauges, gnash snorkels, watching for the blink, where I sweep all with my tidal eyelids. They could be my diving brides never to wed. But I hold out, stare against flipper tickle, all for my beautiful explorers.

Short Hair bows, secures guideline, takes her time. Blondie unsheathes knife from ankle clip. She slices my cornea, and through the slit Short Hair kicks, thigh-thrumming ingress, into pupil gloom, brushing black walls with gloved fingertips. Blondie repeats the incision, then jumps in her chosen eye, the left one. I feel them swallowed, the guideline deadly slack. I blink to remind them how much they are loved, missed, wishing for safe return to surface, to my vision, my selfish need to see the outside of things.

Down they go, down where light traps, where sight squeezes, in search of rods and cones, ocular bullion glinting like doubloons. These diving pioneers will be first to witness what witnessed them. I vow to look only into darkness, beckoning their ascent through widened pupils—anatomy as a hole, an absence.

Blondie gets greedy, hugs an armful of rods, drops like a lead cataract. Her air chokes out, but Short Hair shares her regulator. Her pearls of mercy-breath trickle in my blind spot. I hope they return, or they'll burn corpses in my retinas. I could never look at light again.

FATHER'S KNOTS

Father huffs gnarled German-English into the boy's ear. "I will teach you der Knoten," he says. His hands curl and kink like vulture talons. He loops lengths of rope with corpse grip. The boy gazes above Father's brutal knuckles, where airplanes lace smoke across the red dusk. Crisp white airplanes so much better than his bobbing, mildewed boat hull.

"Watch now," Father says. "The test will follow." Father lashes cord in a fury, despite his Dupuytren's contracture. Some bull scheisse disease, his father always says, will never slow him. His pinkie is latched to palm, middle and ring twisted, doubled-over defeated thumb. These fingers will never straighten from the claw, but that is fine for knot tying. A utilitarian crippling.

"This we call the Sheepshank," Father says. "Now the Turk's Kopf." And the boy ponders names to give Father's fingers: fallen towers, cat-o-five tail. "The Angler's Loop," Father says, "appears complicated." He lifts the pale hemp fibers against the red sky, and the airplane disappears behind a cloud. "Not complicated— beautiful." Father says, "Der Angler is easy."

He ties it again and again, yanking cords from his pockets, then plucking loose rigging from the deck. "A cinch," Father says. "Ein kleiner joke for you." He circles the boy, loops his feet, his thighs, his wrists, his neck. The brined fibers rake his skin.

Father leaves the boy two fingers free on each hand.

33

He slaps his cheeks, says, "If you watched closely, then you will escape der Knoten. But you will never escape these." Father rubs his mangled middle finger against the boy's nose. "Yours will be the same one day."

The boy squirms, makes no progress. Father's knots are perfect. How long will Father leave him? Until he's mastered the Angler or starves, or until all the planes crash from the sky, splash into the sea and capsize Father's boat. The boy longs to stretch his palms, uncrease his lifeline that stretches just as long as Father's. But this will not happen. He couldn't follow the grotesque ballet of Father's crippled fingers, and now Father saunters toward the cabin, whistling dead Mother's lullaby. The lullaby she sang to the boy. Stolen. Her long, straight fingers he used to suck. Gone. Now he has all the time to wait for the clouds to part, for the airplane to reappear, the Angler cord to wither and fray. Inside the ropes, he practices the future, clenches his young fingers into a gnarl like Father's.

THE PLUMBER WHO FOUND TREASURE

The holes in Jane's shoes seeped the rain that streamed down the sleek asphalt of Ruby Lane. Her feet squished along the rows of dark Tudors built on spec. Her pockets were empty, save for matches and the picture of her daughter she kept stowed in a plastic baggie. She hadn't seen her in two months, since entering KPEP Correctional, where the women slept in bunks and traded cigarettes and were released for work and thanked their higher powers they weren't quite in jail. Jane might've preferred jail, which was cheaper, which didn't require anger management meetings, the Life Enhancing Decision Series, or those big twelve steps. Every session meant bills stacking up in her husband's mailbox printed with the numbers 4358, a number she no longer called home.

Jane trudged down Sapphire Drive, to the end of its cul-de-sac, the fields of wild pines bordered by more grandiose spec houses. She tucked her chin into her chest, hid her eyes from houses she'd helped build up until last year alongside her husband. She'd gotten him the job hanging drywall, even though he had zero experience. Now he had the job, and she no longer got to claim the title of the only woman plumber on site. There were hardly any plumbing jobs to be had anymore, and the houses they'd built were rotting in wait for home buyers who now seemed dead as dinosaurs.

When she lifted her chin, the three-story house in the middle of the cul-de-sac stared back at her, its columned porch beckoning her out of the rain like an open palm. Jane climbed the porch steps. She took out the baggie protecting her daughter. She was four in the picture, wore a mermaid costume with a bright red wig and smiled so hard it looked like her teeth could shatter. Under the picture, Jane fished out her last bent cigarette. She thanked her higher power for good carpentry, vinyl siding, a dry porch. Her higher power, she'd decided in KPEP, was a giant, glowing mermaid who was always nodding, nodding and swishing her golden tail. They'd tried to coax her against choosing a giant mermaid in favor of Jesus Christ or Allah or Buddha or the amorphous blankness of simply A Higher Power. She preferred the mermaid.

Jane lit her cigarette, and the matchhead gleamed off the chrome doorknob, the lockbox slung over it. It was the only light she'd seen since stalking the Treasure Springs subdivision. It seemed a sign. Jane punched in the old code they used when she'd worn an American Plumber T-shirt instead of the soaked Hard Rock T-shirt she wore now. 1-2-3-4, a code she was sure they'd changed. The lockbox clicked, and a key tinkled to the floorboards. She burned a second match, and the silver key winked at her.

Inside the oak door, Jane praised her golden mermaid for giving her a dry cavern of a house to sleep in with plush Berber carpets and water flowing from faucets and not the sky and even electricity she found when she flicked the light switches. Cobwebs crowded the ceiling corners. A long crack zigzagged between the big south windows on the living room wall. She flicked off the light. The house was a splendid cavern again. Twenty-foot ceilings her giant mermaid could fit inside and have room to swish her tail.

Jane fumbled to the basement, into richer darkness. Her breaths filled the hard silence of cinderblocks and concrete. Lightning sparked through the egress windows and flashed against the copper plumbing. Her plumbing, her work from five years ago. Lightning sparked again and the brass fittings flickered. She closed her eyes and could still see the maze of plumbing in purple streaks.

36

She found the shutoff valve, twisted it tight, ran up the stairs and turned on the faucets throughout the house, let the water bleed out. The sky mimicked the plumbing, both slowing to a drizzle. She thanked the giant, golden mermaid for agreeing with her plan.

Back in the basement, she gripped a copper pipe above her, gently tugged, and a length of copper broke free. The solders and fasteners snapped like fish bones. Too easy. The house wanted her to have its pipes, had no use for such things when it was just a house missing its people. No family, no home.

Jane stripped all she could carry. She loaded her arms with pipes, pockets with fittings, and then locked the house. She bowed on the porch, told the house she would be back, after she scrapped the copper and brass, filled her baggie with a few grams. She'd return and fix up the spec house, fill it with her daughter on the weekends, for Halloween even, and she'd wear her mermaid costume and knock on all the neighborhood's grand oak doors that would have people inside suddenly.

Jane wanted to get out the picture of her daughter again, but her arms were too full of treasure. So she thanked her giant, glowing mermaid, and then slogged away down Sapphire Drive.

A BETTER TRAP

A neck snaps as my daughter sleeps. She is one year old. I've killed five mice. This time, I find the trap licked clean of peanut butter bait, and I'm glad to have provided a last meal. I long to extend mercy, but my daughter lives here, sleeps open-mouthed here, eats here, mashes her face into the carpet. Or maybe this mouse didn't get a last meal, and instead its kin lapped up the peanut butter before its dying eyes. I understand the cruelty of survival. How delicate that string of pink mouse tongue must have been, thin as unblown dandelion seeds, the ones my daughter can't yet dislodge, more spit than wind passing through her lips. Same with candles—spit-speckling her cake as she chants "Happy Tuesday to you." The "birth" has been lost, and it sounds like we're celebrating a weekday. We marvel at the wonder of Tuesday.

The colony learns to elude the wire traps, and I'm glad to give up the old traps that sometimes misfire and purple my thumbnail. The walls click and scratch at night. I purchase a better mouse-trap—durable plastic, shark-toothed, guaranteed, a snap to set—to protect my thumbnails, to protect my daughter. But under the oven, it melts after one baked Happy Tuesday cake. The plastic shark teeth wilt and warp, are in need of braces. I buy another better mousetrap. My daughter sleeps as I collect half a dozen mice, dumping corpses and re-smearing last-meal bait. The walls go silent.

Later, while walking my dog, daughter backpacked behind me, I encounter a mouse scuttling against the curb, trajectory aimed at our house. It is slow, bumbling. I could easily stomp it.

Instead, I nudge it with the toe of my shoe until it aims in the opposite direction. Perhaps a neighbor's house. Better to live anywhere but here.

ON THE STRONGEST MAN COMPOUND

In the deepest deserts of Regular Man World hides the lush, AstroTurfed oasis of the Strongest Man Compound. There the Strongest Men are getting ripped, benching '55 Ford chasses, curling telephone poles, squatting trailer homes. The Strongest Men are getting huge. All except one Strongest Man, Harold, who is shrinking. Yesterday, he beat the compound record by benching 979.5 pounds, plus the weight of two Strongest Men clinging to the bar. As soon as he hoisted those cheering Strongest Men into the air, his biceps deflated from massive watermelons to slightly less massive watermelons. The Strongest Men shrugged it off, chalked it up to muscle tone. When Harold beat the record for pushups, thrusting his rebar spine up through the night and into the pink dawn, his decreasing size became a larger concern. As the sun split over the cacti-dotted desert and Harold collapsed under his 26,353rd pushup, the Strongest Men measured a .65-inch loss in height. The Strongest Men hissed theories at one another on whether he began shrinking due to bad form from the first pushup or an unprecedented burst of lactic acid.

Whatever the cause, Harold was undoubtedly getting smaller, and his diminishing size shocked fear into every Strongest Man flex, every lift, every aching muscle.

Over the next few days, whenever a Strongest Man passed Harold's Power Quadrant, they saw him in action. He skipped all mandatory Meditative Mirror Flexings to grunt out extra chin-ups. Instead of breaking for Protein Replenishment Sessions, Harold slid extra weight onto his bench bar. The Strongest Men mixed him extra protein shakes, took turns dumping them down his throat between reps. When Harold thanked the Strongest Men with high-fives, his slender fingers felt like children's hands against their palms. In his decreasing hours of Power Naps, the Strongest Men crept to his cot, slipped supplements under his doll-like tongue, injected hormones into his delicate forearms. Harold kept getting smaller. The pride of the Strongest Men, the strongest of the strongest, soon stood as tall as their triceps.

When Harold arrived for his newest tattoos, the Strongest Tattooist noted how Harold's curly blond hair waved below his deltoids. It reminded him of his daughter at home, far away, aging quickly, whose tears had wetted his upper abs the last time they hugged goodbye. If he were home now, she'd be tall enough to weep into his pectorals.

The Strongest Tattooist set to work inking a new barb around Harold's right bicep, as he did for every Strong Man when they completed a new feat of strength. The Strongest Tattooist swept Harold's long hair behind his ear, smiled, and then squinted in horror at his masterpiece. The decreasing bicep surface area and exponentially increased output of feats morphed Harold's rugged barbed-wire trophies into a prickly accordion ink clump. The Strongest Tattooist took a deep breath, closed his eyes, remembered the time his daughter dropped a dumbbell on his red inks which spattered all over his white walls. He'd swallowed a roar and the disappointment chasing it. They'd spent the rest of the day together, flicking red ink patterns at the walls. They found delight in disaster. So the Strongest Tattooist expanded his canvas, ringing barbed bands from deltoids to finger flexors. The other Strongest Men would think Harold was becoming striped, but the Strongest Tattooist would think of his daughter and their ink-spattered walls.

The Strongest Men held a meeting once they confirmed they could wrap a hand around Harold's quads. They convened in the Vascularity Tent, its ceiling draped with purple velvet and its walls crammed with three-way mirrors. One Strongest Man arched his shoulders into the mirror and suggested stilts. Another Strongest Man gritted his teeth, flexed his triceps in a triangle, and suggested a padded sweat suit made of red suede with gold trimming. The Strongest Men nodded, thought that would look ruggedly regal.

The Strongest Tattooist raised one finger, wanted to urge against hiding his tattoos under so much fabric. But their meeting ended when Harold lifted the Vascularity Tent into the air.

"Count my reps, boys," Harold shouted from outside the velvet tent flaps.

"This can't go on," one Strongest Man pledged while tumbling across the floor mats.

"Thirty-five, thirty-six, thirty-seven," the Strongest Tattooist chanted to Harold. "He is our brother, and we must always spot him."

A third Strongest Man braced himself, palms pressed against two sides of his three-way mirror. "We have reputations to consider. Just look at us," he said while he gazed at his flexed delts, "and look at him."

The Strongest Men commissioned the Strongest Tailor to cut the finest sweat suit ever made. He stuffed the suit with so much sculpted padding that even the most Regular Man could slip inside and appear Strongest-Man-buff. But the Strongest Men couldn't coax Harold into the finest sweat suit. They presented it to him during crunches, and Harold gave a thumbs-up between his 654th and 655th sit-up. He didn't stop crunching. The sweat suit grew heavy in the Strongest Men's outstretched hands. Their smiles drooped. Their arms quavered under the weight of mere fabric. They followed Harold all day as he strained his ever-diminishing muscles. He sprinted between each set, from one end of the compound to another, and the Strongest Men scurried after, dragging the limp legs of the finest sweat suit over the AstroTurf until the hems frayed.

The Strongest Men voted in the United States of Strength Hut whether they should exile Harold. The vote passed thirty-seven to twenty-three. They planned a Strongest Man human pyramid to reach the top of the fence and dispel him into the Regular Man World. But Harold shrank to two feet tall and slipped through their oiled legs and onto his next workout. The Strongest Men still constructed their pyramid, each man's muscles gleaming in the setting sun, and they symbolically tossed Harold's duffle bag over the fence. It puffed against the desert dust. The Strongest Tattooist crouched on all fours at the bottom of the pyramid and imagined his daughter's legs growing long, pressing her feet against a gas pedal and speeding her tall frame down the freeway. He dropped tears he hoped the others would mistake for sweat.

The USS Hut remained bulging with Strongest Men every evening as they passed further Harold-inhibitive legislation. The inevitable vote finally came. Harold had to die. It was the only way to stop his tragic anti-sizing and preserve the memory of his mass. The next matter to face voting was the method of execution. One Strongest Man suggested hanging. The other Strongest Men shook their heads vigorously. Hanging was an execution used on Regular Men and Strongest Men deserved extraordinary ends. They debated firing squads and alligator pits, electrocution and implosion, elephant trampling and flamethrowers.

The Strongest Tattooist listened while he sketched barbed-wire calligraphy to stripe Harold's thigh, a leg so short it probably wouldn't reach his daughter's kneecaps. She stretched across his memory, gazelle legs, a giraffe neck extending into some distant lush tree line. He knew desert best now, and Harold's body, his shrinking masterpiece. He wondered how tiny it could shrink. The Strongest Tattooist squeezed his fingers into great fists and ground them into his vein-swathed forehead. He uttered through his forearms, "We end him with weight. It's the only respectable thing to do. More weight than ever has been lifted."

The Strongest Men nodded their vascular brows. They'd discovered the proper way to eradicate their champion.

The Strongest Men spent the next three days gathering stacks of dumbbells and barbells, hundreds of steel donuts and free weights, all the Ford chasses and telephone poles, boulders and tractor tires, even the two-pound pink dumbbells the Strongest Tailor used to strengthen his pinky fingers. The Strongest Carpenter dismantled the studs and siding of the USS Hut and added it to the weight pile. They gathered their cots, weight benches and regular benches. They filled their duffle bags and all wore only their gray casual speedos. The Strongest Men stripped their compound bare and piled everything on the mountain of weight.

The day arrived when there was no more weight. The Strongest Men paced, hands in pockets, muscles involuntarily flexing. All that was left was to call Harold, but none could do it. They all hugged their barbed biceps and gazed at the Strongest Tattooist's feet. He hesitated, but it had been his idea. His daughter, in her speeding car, would never hesitate, would throttle onward. He shouted, "This is surely the greatest feat of strength ever known to Strongest Men."

The Strongest Men flashed their polished teeth as Harold approached their pile and whistled. He looked like a figurine next to the mountain of weight. "Now that's a weight only a Strongest Man could lift," Harold said on cue, as if a string in his back had been pulled.

The Strongest Tattooist answered that it was a weight only *The* Strongest Man could lift, that man being Harold, and he'd saved a special ink, the blackest midnight of blacks, for the man who could lift it. The Strongest Men all nodded. They smiled wider and wider. They didn't know that the Strongest Tattooist actually had gathered the blackest midnight of black inks, that he secretly hoped he'd succeed. He marveled at the tiny barbs on Harold's striped body that he couldn't create with his bulky fingers, and he spied the last blank flesh on Harold's left calf with aching fingertips.

"Load me up, boys," Harold said, flicking the USS Hut's subfloor onto his shoulders.

The Strongest Men stacked their beloved weight. The Strongest Tattooist flattened his abs against the AstroTurf to monitor Harold under the subfloor. Harold, darkened by shadows, his tattoos blurred, winked as his feet sank into the AstroTurf. The Strongest Men scavenged more weight: their dirty laundry, their picture frames of Mr. Universe and back issues of *Muscle Man*, wall mirrors and hand mirrors, jugs of protein powder. They built the mountain, item by item, with huge heaving chests and vein-popping forearms, until the Strongest Tattooist waved one arm from the ground. He squinted into the inch of darkness under the subfloor, but couldn't see Harold.

"Need a spot down there, Harold?" the Strongest Men asked, snickering.

"Is that all there is?" Harold answered like a far-off whisper.

Only the Strongest Tattooist smiled. But there was always more weight. They ripped the AstroTurf from the ground. They yanked the cyclone fence and added that, too. They scooped boulders, armfuls of earth.

The Strongest Tattooist heard Harold wheeze from the darkness. The Strongest Men climbed atop the mountain and added their own bodies, the purest weight of flesh. The mountain shuddered, shook, and then it plummeted exactly one quarter of an inch.

The Strongest Tattooist called to Harold, but he didn't answer. He yelled louder. He pressed his lips into the mountain and bellowed Harold's name over and over until he couldn't remember any other name. His daughter was zooming through a green world, so tall she floated into the sky, took flight, stretched giant and air-thin. Every cloud became her image. He clawed at the ground, but found nothing. The tiniest Strongest Man was no more.

The Strongest Men puzzled over the mountain of weight in the following days. They couldn't remember the layout of the compound, where each hut and tent and workout station and flex area had stood. The AstroTurf shriveled in the hot son, and the cyclone fence lay snarled like a mess of tangled barbed wire.

The Strongest Men looked at each other's arms and couldn't remember who had completed which feat, what Strongest Job they'd held. The compound was all parched earth and slack muscles and gray casual speedos. They wandered into the desert, into Regular Man World. The wind whispered into their ears, just above their delts, called for them to find more weight. But they couldn't remember what was weight and what wasn't. They shambled toward one cloud that looked like a long woman spread across the sky.

HAIR CROPPER SHIES

Neither of us is happy, Farmer Hanley. A tough year for follicles atop my head, where you work. You cringe at other crops, passing high, plateaus of wealth, healthy scalps, neighbors smiling for snapshots, bowing next to their behemoth locks, junior perched on top, gapped front teeth like an oil well, black and oozing. Our barren bald spot blinks its betrayal. The neighbors see, suck in lips, click tongues, say, "How his hair is growing thin." No thicket to hide in, your overall buttons flash rescue through sparse stalks. But I can't save you, or me, nor can the almanac you tried to take back, slogged with rain and useless predictions. Hide in your browning combine to thresh futility—dust bowl, Rustbelt, recession of hairlines. You close your eyes and circle my scalp, seedless plow lines. Pray you find one bale, pray you find anything, before blue skies shade pink, the embarrassing naked of windswept clouds parting above our hairlines. Then head home, where Wife washes flatware in a stainless-steel basin, blazing sparks through the kitchen window.

POSTAL HETEROCHROMIA

The postman glares with his green eye, then his blue. He nods at the next in line, waves, coaxes with one curled finger. But the woman in front is frozen, can't decide what to send where. She hugs a dozen boxes, shuffles three more across the linoleum. The corners are crushed, blackened, the packing tape slack. This ballet of boxes is going nowhere.

The postman calls them parcels, not boxes. He sucks his mustache and calculates weight by eye. One green, one blue. Everyone asks how it happened. Stab wound? Poison? Dropped as an infant? Cancer or cataract? Luck, he tells them. Since birth, a whole life, they've always been this way, two-toned and terrifying. Together, his eyes bully cowed customers into ordering insurance and tracking and two-day delivery. They cannot deny the wretch with two different eyes.

The woman at the front of the line feels them boring into her boxes, x-raying the insides. She wants him to see, to guess the purpose of her parcels. She doesn't know herself, wishes someone would guess and be wrong and then she'd be closer to knowing what to do with her husband's chalky remains. A shoddy cremation left her with shards instead of flakes. Knob of knee, knuckle joint, elbow ulna, eye socket curves that once held two brown eyes, perfectly equal. These pieces are recognizable, but not enough to piece him back together, to make a skeleton, like the one looming in the corner of her high school biology classroom, like the one in the postman's high school biology classroom, like the one in the high school biology classroom of every person who ever stood in line at this post office waiting for a woman who couldn't decide where to send parts she recognized not quite enough.

Come forward, begs the postman's two different eyes. Just come forward, out of that line, and I will help. He knows where everything goes that doesn't fit. He'll randomize zip codes, from Miami to Tacoma. He'll dispatch her husband's pieces so kindly, so long as she doesn't ask what happened to his eyes.

THE OUIJA BOARD INSPECTOR

On that cursed day when we ruined Wallace Cotts, the Ouija board inspector, we'd gathered near the sanding station to watch him press his ear to the glossy box top. He began each inspection this way, by listening to cardboard hollows for the spirits within. Next, he used his pinky fingers to gentle the top free. He fanned the new box aroma toward his nose, filled his lungs and closed his eyes and balanced on one leg. Then, with eyes still closed, he grazed fingertips against the planchette's point. He kissed the talking board's right corner to sample the tang of fresh lacquer.

We, the women of the Ouija board assembly line, have always been the true heart behind production, the ink renderers, wood finishers, lacquer perfectionists. But Wallace claimed only he could unleash the everlasting entanglement. "Even simple assembly labor," he told us while clutching Fiona's callused hands between his silk gloves, "can achieve the ethereal realms of greatness thanks to my talents."

Maybe we wouldn't have minded him so much if Marge hadn't asked his hourly wage, if he hadn't told us, without hesitation, $29.50 next to our $9.35. We expect our seventy-eight cents on the dollar. We plan lives around injustice that rolls down every assembly line across this nation—forced to work on Christmas Eve, the foreman eyeing our legs during Shorts Fridays in summer, zip for childcare, zilch for healthcare, and Fiona hasn't seen a doctor in ten years since one time when she had no choice. Wallace's $29.50 just tasted more bitter than the burnt breakroom coffee.

Maybe we could've even dealt with the pay if the foreman hadn't bellowed about low productivity levels. We pointed toward the logjam at Wallace's station. His quality control dictated our rate of production, and he had twenty-six boxes stacked around him. The foreman said he'd dock our pay a quarter for every box under quota and then walked right by Wallace, who was chanting on one leg.

Wallace noticed us watching, his eyes meeting ours as his tongue flicked at a freshly lacquered moon on the talking board. He winked.

He was supposed to check for the planchette's glide against the board, that it was smooth as ice, that we'd lacquered evenly and generously, that we sanded away any burrs on the wooden planchette. But quality control of earthly materials hardly concerned him, and we never missed a burr anyway. How disappointing to travel the ethereal planes to land on a maple slab. The least we could do was keep a brave voyager from getting a sliver. Wallace cared only about access. He'd lectured us in the breakroom, while we downed our second burnt coffees and he was still swirling his Formosa red tea. "Give it your best, girls, and I'll make the spirits sing."

Board after board, he was reaching into the void, he preached, like dredging a pond to test its depth before diving. Some he found too shallow, the planchette stubborn, the talking board short on words, and what joy could be had in wading a kiddie pool? Others opened up like oceans, endless eddies tugging his soul as the planchette zagged from letter to letter. These boards he marked for devolumizing; three extra coats of lacquer usually muffled the roar. Something about the lacquer layers, a direct relationship between sheen and spirit. The muted boards, though, those useless kiddie pools, he tossed directly into the trash. We'd keep the box, sneak the planchettes into our pockets. Our foreman monitored the trash bin with regular skepticism, but never complained to Wallace, only tallied up our pay docking. It was the inspector's spiritual finesse, Wallace claimed, that kept our small-fish company from being swallowed by Hasbro. Anyone could spread ink. Anyone could carve a planchette. Only he, Grand Sorcerer of $29.50 Bullshit, was irreplaceable.

Maybe our revenge had something to do with the ridiculous boxes featuring Wallace's picture on the front. The Ouija circuit and séance nuts knew him well. He donned the same getup at work that was featured on the box: black bowler cap, purple cape, pinstriped button-down. We wore the same navy-blue polos and pale jeans. While we stowed our hair in nets, our eyes behind safety glasses, he sported a monocle on a pink-gold chain to peer through the planchette's window.

Our pictures would never show up on a box. But sometimes, while we waited for Wallace, all of us penned our initials on the box's inside. We hid our letters in a tiny corner. Wallace never noticed, and some kid would someday think she'd received secret code from the beyond. It's us, kids, the women from the line who truly make the spirits sing.

On the day of his ruin, his head tipped back to expose his vein-strained neck. His eyes rolled to whiteness as he channeled the dead. Nothing new, of course. He hummed something minor key and melodic. Marge guessed either "House of the Rising Sun" or Bach's Fifth. Then Wallace initiated communing. His mom was his usual go-to first contact. We take solace knowing that when we someday die, we'll finally have some time with our kids, though we pitied Wallace's pestered mother. He called to her in a nagging chant, *mothermothermothermother*. He asked her who she watched *Jeopardy* with last night, her favorite post-mortem leisure activity. He asked if she was fighting with Agnes, who was apparently her roommate in death, which disappointed us since we all hoped to be unburdened by leases and cohabitation. He communicated with the maternal afterlife loud enough for our benefit: "Oh, dear Mother, of course I know you're proud. I miss you, too, but take heart in knowing your son's budding legacy."

Next, he tuned to Javier. This rarely happened, only on good boards, on good days. Javier had died on the factory line when they used to make jeans here. Javier was always aggressive in his possession. Wallace's spine contorted in sporadic seizures. Javier shouted for someone to wrench him from the riveter, and then he screamed for his wife. To tell her what, Wallace didn't bother to reveal.

But on the last day, Wallace dove deeper, past Javier, into undiscovered loss. The foreman even entered the floor to watch when Wallace fell silent and dropped to his knees. He dragged his pinstriped belly across the floor. He slithered and writhed and babbled, overtaken by a spirit too strong for him. Fiona lurched to lift him from the floor, to soothe his crying, but we held her back.

Maybe we hadn't really expected anything to happen. We'd just grown tired of Wallace's breakroom lectures and sloth-paced production levels, tired of the foreman taking out on us women what was a fault of the single man on the assembly floor. Really, it was more like an experiment than malicious intent. The day prior, while waiting for Wallace to inspect two dozen boxes at his bottleneck, we pricked our fingers and bled one drop each into the ink, then printed the letters with pressed palms and prayers. We each spit into the lacquer and then whispered the name of our most beloved befallen—grandmothers and daddies and lovers and best dogs. We rubbed the box against our throats for good luck. The planchette we held against each our hearts for a full five-minute smoke break. We applied the lacquer thin as air, almost nothing to guard Wallace from our crafting.

Wallace lost the ability to walk that day, to talk, to hold his bowels. His eyes bulged wide as he seemed to discover his hands for the first time, his feet, the lights, the walls, the conveyor belt—all of it seemed a nightmarish wonder to him. He gurgled and tottered on his back, tried to escape his immobility. They say he gave up on the Ouija circuit after that. Sold his monocle and cape on eBay. He works a call center now selling medical braces, making minimum wage plus commission.

And we subsist on the line. The same Ouija boards crank out, but now without hindrance. The foreman hides in his office, terrified to touch our boards. He can't dock our pay any longer, and he gave us each a fifteen-cent raise to keep our mouths shut about Wallace. But what would we say when we know too much?

On Wallace Cotts's last day, we became more powerful than a corporate necromancer. The spirit we'd welcomed plunged deeper than ocean floor. We carried suspicions but couldn't confirm until we picked the lock and studied the security camera footage. There, in grainy detail, we could just make out the planchette's choreography atop the board where we knew the placement of every letter better than our own skin. He spelled out "B-A-B" and then his jaw opened to "Y." Next the letters "Q" and then "U" and then "I" and then "N" and a final "N," and that's where he stopped. We knew the name that had almost been given by the one of us who'd almost given it. Fiona had taken the experiment too seriously, had clutched the planchette too tightly, had poured her beloved into this labor, and no man could handle a spirit heavy as that.

PITCH

The deck salesman opens his customer's slider, bares his upturned palm, and ushers her onto her own deck, saying, "Imagine yourself lounging, an Arnold Palmer in one hand, fan in the other, on your new Ultra-Syntho-Balsa deck, but of course you wouldn't even need a fan if you ordered our Remote-Laxer-Awning, which will ensure that the sun never burns your eyes, that a single drop of sweat never crests your brow, never seeps between your lips to sting your tongue, because all Remote-Laxer-Awnings come equipped with personal climate control coolers, which offer so much more than your old, rattling air-conditioner, for these truly condition your atmosphere, lowering not only the temperature—because a perfect seventy-one degrees is only a number—but raising the subatomic serenity of surrounding air molecules which will imbue the corresponding electrons with a state of perpetual quantum giddiness, like when you were seven and you fell in love with Zander, the next-door neighbor, who promised to marry you and buy you three ponies and four cows and seven sheep because he came from a family that never worried about money like yours did, his father the most successful realtor in town, and Zander took you to the big vacant house down the street, a home no one could afford, but the two of you deserved it and plotted where the horse stables would be, and Zander taught you what a kiss felt like and then you played doctor but you didn't worry about bodies then because this was innocent love, and how joyous your lungs will feel when absorbing a perfectly controlled climate, the fullest breaths you've ever taken, whereas your breaths now are stifled half-inhales, muffled gasps, which I see you're doing now, and that's because you're uncomfortable on this deck, this sun-soaked, sweltering calamity of rusted screws and warped boards which prove that wood, real wood, is an obsolete relic, as absurdly antiquated as one of those vibrating exercise belt things, you know, the ones you wrap around your buttocks and then flip on the motor and it shakes you silly, and, if we're being honest, doesn't really make you any more appealing to your husband who comes home lugging a briefcase, wearing an overcoat and a porkpie hat and a crooked necktie and he barely glances at you before he drives to the bar to find a lady of the night and forget about your C-section scar and your two beautiful children, Wallace and Sarah, those beautiful children who split open your belly, and now they've forgotten about you, thank you for nothing, won't even invite you to their air-conditioned homes during this heatwave where you may very well faint and cook in your lawn chair, lost in searing dreams for a simple, quick, easy solution that you damn-well earned, yet this Sears-Roebuck-catalog world has disappointed you with its jokes of innovation, but, of course, this is only a fictionalized scenario I'm using to illustrate how important it is that we follow sincere innovations and not rely on snake-oil promises, and I certainly don't mean to say your body is repulsive, your husband unloving, your kids ungrateful, but I would definitely say your deck is in dire need of an upgrade, and no matter the state of your marital bliss, my company, Decks for Life, guarantees at least three increments of life improvement, including the soothing of your over-worked feet against our patented Syntho-Balsa grain, and your sun-strained eyes will be protected by our retractable awning decorated by fiber-optic fabrics that emulate the shifting clouds you watched on your back with Billy Upshaw who you loved after Zander and his constant demands to play doctor, and wasn't Billy's love purer, unspoiled by bodily desire, by the boys inching their clammy fingers up your tensed thighs, and you'll look up, sipping your Arnold Palmer, and you'll ask the ghost of Billy, who died

58

fighting for our country before he ever even gave you a kiss, Does that look like an elephant to you? and the ghost of Billy will reply, Yes, yes, that fiber-optically simulated cloud does look like an elephant, an elephant carrying on its back a Pegasus on the verge of soaring far, far away to some place like Uruguay or Kathmandu, and those places sound so lovely slipping over your tongue, but in reality, ma'am, those places are dirty and poor, and they don't carry our awnings or decks, and thus shouldn't be visited, and you're much better off staying exactly where you are, so long as you upgrade your deck, which will only require forty-six easy payments, but judging by your deck perhaps you'd like our Extended Comfort Payment Plan which consists of ninety-seven even easier payments, and there's no shame in that, and you'll still have the deck paid off before this house that you bought on a thirty-year mortgage, when you and your husband were in your thirties and you both had wonderful new careers, he as a junior executive for General Motors and you as an Avon saleswoman, but then he deemed your income frivolous when you could be raising his children and folding his underwear and dressing in lacy lingerie every night, and the thigh-high garters dug into your skin, as did the straps of your brassiere to keep your breasts floating high, nipples aimed to the sky, and your shoulders burned and blistered and then, finally, he made love to you quickly, in harsh thrusts, before flopping onto his back and crying silently an hour later because in twenty years GM would be laying him off and you'd need to return to work, because there's always work for a saleswoman, indeed there is, and I know that you know what I know—these tricks we use to sell, to promise that every aspect of life will improve if you just buy or else suffer the regret of what could've been—and I don't underestimate your knowledge, so let's be straight with each other: this deck is still just a deck, but it is a better deck, and something you desperately need, if for no other reason than to make you smile and shake your head every time you slide open the door and look at that beautiful new, completely unnecessary deck and you think, Goddamn that salesman who got me to pull the trigger, who broke the code and shed the pitch and bared his honesty, nude and raw, but that is the kind of man who deserves my attention, not the liars who promised me a better life while aching for my attention, my body, my sacrifice, and it's all a kind of cruelty, ma'am, which I clearly understand, so I'll guarantee that this deck will bring you no happiness, except for the revenge you desire to spite Billy and Zander and your husband, who will all be awed (some posthumously) by your investment in your personal satisfaction, and they'll think twice next time before making ridiculous promises they can't provide, because all you ever really wanted was someone who will tell you the truth and stop pretending that love will simply cure all, will fix anything, and was there ever a better sales pitch than love's panacea, so will you please accept this brochure at the very least and place it under your pillow and toss and turn over this grave decision until you finally decide to run off with me to Uruguay where we won't live happily ever after."

TO WAIT FOR LANDING

We brought cans of beer embossed with silver mountains, as many as we could steal from Toby's dad's fridge and stash in our coat pockets. We carried our cargo down 89 to a tight dirt road that dead-ended at the small airport outside our town of cornfields. From the trunk of Conner's '82 Crown Vic, we pulled four flimsy green lawn chairs and set them in a half-circle at midnight to scout for planes. We waited almost every night. Seamus said drug runners used the tiny airstrip to smuggle in massive shipments of high-grade pot, that if we ever saw a plane land, they'd gift garbage bags of the stuff to keep our mouths shut. It happened to one of his brother's friends six years ago. It could happen to us.

We planned to have beer waiting for them. The drug runners would guzzle, the tracks of red and white airstrip lights glinting around silver cans suckled by their chapped, nerve-shattered lips. We'd be their heroes. They'd be ours.

Though a single plane never landed on our watch, we vowed to wait, forever if needed, to see the airstrip burst into light. Our wasted time was worth any chance.

One night in August, when Toby was grounded for stealing beers, and Conner was fixing his radiator, and Seamus was writing a makeup essay about *Hamlet* so he could barely graduate in the summer—I brought a girl to our airport. I drove her in my father's new Silverado. We didn't have lawn chairs or beer, but we sipped from an unlabeled bottle half-filled with whiskey. I told her our plans about planes. Our backs smothered the cool grass, our feet propped against the chain-link surrounding the airstrip. Her toes curled the wire knots while I spilled everything. I nudged her shoulder, and she swallowed the last drop.

As I considered plans for my lips to touch hers, to finally cash in my summer of waiting at the airport, a row of white lights snapped on in the distance. I bolted upright, my lips cool and dry. Another row of white, then red, sketched paths over a black field. I scoured the sky. I ached for engine hum. I reached for a lawn chair that wasn't there to steady my legs. She chucked the bottle over the fence, onto the strip, where it didn't break. An hour later and still no plane, no landing, no drug runners, no lovers, just the two of us clinging fence—my fingers, her toes.

She got bored, and I drove her home. I never told the guys what I didn't see, and they'd never know they missed lights carving the dark field. I'll never know if a plane sputtered overhead that night. They were lucky to not have come so close. Had Seamus and Toby and Conner been there, we would have waited all night, for whole days, the rest of our summers.

THE DIVINER

She grips her hickory rod like a Y-shaped whisper. Her bare feet glide across my tongue, my softest muscle mashed under her callused heels. Her gray-blue eyes and her black curls warble light and loose as her rod grip—that rod that refuses to rock, to drop, to find a spot. I promise there is water here inside my mouth. I just drank, emptied an empty soda can refilled with holy water from the city assessor's office drinking fountain, where the maps crinkle like ten thousand wind chimes, and the water is coppery and endless and I drank and I drank. So I know there is water. I promise water. Her eyelids drip shut.

She says she does her best dowsing blind, silent, with a numb tongue and a dumb ear. Senseless is the way to find the spring under the rock. The rock my dry tongue which I swear was once wet. I can't seem to salivate. I haven't tasted an apple in four years, an orange in five, a nectarine ever. I never did like fruit.

But there is water here. I assure her. I am sure I feel the twitch of her rod dipping, dowsing, the pendulum of twig finding root in me, my mouth, my tongue. She says no. She says you must learn to decipher true dip from a slipped grip.

She—this flake of spirit wearing an unbleached, all-natural, pesticide-free, blinding white cotton dress—is fallible, she assures me. But her rod never errs. Hickory doesn't know how to lie.

My tongue, my mouth, my whole body—mostly water and carbon, a couple pounds of phosphorous, a pinch of gold. I'm getting off track, she tells me, and this is why I'm dry. I talk too much, won't hear the moment when hickory and skin sing.

ANGEL IN THE PIT

I've seen him at damn near every show wearing that bright-white T-shirt, impossibly unstained. The angel is skinny and tall and his red mohawk spikes in neat thorns. After the show, he looks the same as when he walked in—perfect, except for the sweat beads that burst into prisms on his shaved scalp.

Everywhere I go—Circle Jerks in Cincinnati, Bad Religion in Detroit, when the floor fell out at The Local, Descendants in Chicago, The Slits in Indianapolis—he's there. When that skinhead crashed red crystals out of beer bottle and some kid's skull, the angel wrapped the kid's head up with duct tape, not a blot of blood on his shirt. That was at the house party with MDC. But when SNFU opened for NOFX, he fished a pair of glasses and a wallet from the pit and returned them to their rightful owners. I'd like to imagine doing the same, but I would've stomped the glasses, ganked the cash. And my shirt always yellows, blotches, wrinkles.

When Stiff Little Fingers played Cleveland, I didn't see him all night. I stood by the speakers and let my pants *whish, whish* to the *thump-a-thump* of the kick drum. A pretty girl with blue hair surfed along the crowd packed tight. But Stiff switched it up to a reggae number—*unchaka, unchaka*. The crowd fanned out. The girl balanced on a few last fingertips, tipped, descended. The angel showed up, his red mohawk charging like a rhino horn. Flash of white. She floated in his arms. I watched from the bar.

She stood, they stared, locked eyes, slow-danced in the pit like it was prom. It was empty around them. No bodies. Nobody to break their sway—*chaka, unchaka, bada-boom boom da-boom.*

And even when Stiff picked it up, pulsing and pounding, the crowd parted around them. An oasis in the pit. Angel and fallen. Stage light of white, blessed circle. Me alone, in the dark, silent and unsaved.

THE MOUTH FULL OF FLYING

I'm at a Rancid show in Pontiac, Michigan. A gothic church turned into a club called Clutch Cargo's. Arches draped in logos. Stained glass and strobe lights. Cigarette butts and angel statues everywhere. The millennium is brand new, and it will be five more years before this half of the state crumbles around its empty factories. Eight more before I use gel for combovers instead of spikes.

The crowd surges. A giant man in boots loops his arms, offers me a boost. I don't feel the crowd's hands lifting me, can't distinguish fingernails or July smoldering outside. It's a furnace of bodies down there. But the air lightens, cools, floating just above exhale and sweat. My lungs fill, sharing the same breath as on that stage—gods with guitars and gaping mouths, red-tipped mohawks piercing smoke clouds. I'm eyelevel with a bluebird tattoo, wings spread, migrating toward the singer's jugular. I'm migrating, too, toward stage. The stratosphere is jealous. Bluebirds are jealous. I'm jealous of dreams where I can fly. And will be forever of this moment when I am light as music, bodiless, sailing distortion and feedback that pulses through strings, through pickups, through speaker, into the input, out the output. I'm phantom hover. I'm all eardrums. Until two of my fingers materialize—made real by the feel of slipping down a hot, choking throat. I'm gagging a man in the crowd. Below me. Was holding me. Long brown hair soaked in sweat, a beard, brown eyes drowning in surprise. If not for the surprise, I would've believed he was Jesus. I yank my fingers from his throat. *Sorry*, that your larynx was my scaffold, that music was heavy in your mouth. *That's okay, man.* I actually hear him over everything, my everything that is eardrums. Tonight they'll riot-ring while I try to sleep. For the rest of my life, this pitch will hiss when I find real silence. I still hear it when I rock my daughter to sleep, louder than her whisper-breath. When I sleep, I switch on the fan, turn up the baby monitor—anything to mask quiet's blare.

The Jesus guy said it was okay. The crowd dropped me near the front of the stage, before a speaker that exorcized my heartbeat and implanted its own. The last time I saw Rancid was in Chicago at a House of Blues. My wife and I watched the crowd from a table, watched the tumbling crowd surfers and seething pit as we ordered microbrew beers, and even this was many years before bald spots and Detroit threatening to sell its paintings to pay pensions, before my daughter and real silence. This Easter, the club reopened as a church.

WHEN WE

When you and I turned into snails, I tore myself from my shell, and we squeezed into yours. We pressed against your spirals and they stabbed my flesh, made me secrete unintentionally. But you laughed it off and scooched over for me.

When we puffed into nebulas, I squinted my cat's eye, compressed every electron, just to see you dancing all the way over there in Cassiopeia. A ripple of nitrogen, blue bubble inside squinting back.

When we were ceramic dinnerware, you were always stacked on top, me at the bottom. I waited six weeks and two days before we were reshuffled just right, before you clinked on top of me.

When we were nails the hammer bent me. They swept me into the dustpan. The hammer swung at you and you jerked your galvanized point three-eighths of an inch to the left, aimed at that stubborn pine knot. You became bent and useless and dustpan bound.

When we were blood cells, we tumbled after each other to the cadence of that ancient drum.

When you were a tamarin, I was a capuchin, and that was a problem. You wore a gold mane, and my beard was stained yellow, my black cap graying. All I had going for me was a clam locked tight.

You yanked it from my fingers, threw it at the rocks. I thought you'd ruined me, but you returned, naked mussel in hand. There was always less meat in those things than I envisioned, a slime slither that when shared left our stomachs groaning.

When we were steel, they pounded you into a sword and molded me into a breastplate. I never thought I'd see you again, until they thrust you into me. They crafted you better—perfect point to pierce lung through a ribcage, but first you had to tear through me.

Do you remember that jar when we were cicadas? I mean, I was headed your way already when they jammed us into that jar. We buzzed so loud I thought the glass would shatter.

Not long after, you were you and I was me. Diner waitress, house painter. You smelled like syrup and fryer grease, and I reeked of paint thinner. We rescued an orange dog and bought a house and filed joint tax returns. And now we smell like us.

INTERSTATE INTESTINE

This wasn't supposed to be fun. We were moving our lives, not taking a road trip. But you had to stop and snap a picture of every polyp, stand before the World's Largest Lodged Corn Kernel, just so you could say you witnessed the gold-gloss skin of this mired giant. It could fill the space between us—the humming gearshift, your skirt hem blotted in yellow stains, because you had to visit the tapeworm petting zoo, appetites larger than every piece of dusty furniture in my truck bed. Everything gets swallowed here. Every last piece of us evaporates. And now where will we sleep? Where will you hide your diary, stow your threadbare underwear old as teenage children? Your underwear is gone, as is your diary, each secret sentence digested down to meaningless letters, even the serifs snapping away. I read your secrets, took notes in a similarly secret diary. My words tracking your words are also lost now. But I remember: You said you'd disappear if I couldn't stop being so serious, so determined not to laugh at all we've lost. Through the rear-view is our empty truck bed, tires spinning in slosh, nothing but knotted, red small intestine walls out the window, a vision unobstructed by you and your stained skirt and digested secrets, because you jumped at the last town, tucked and rolled, gave up on leaving by leaving me.

LONG DIVISION

Hammers make good divisors. When smashing dividends—alarm clock radios or cassette-playing boom boxes or pull-string Pee-wee Herman dolls—remainders are inevitable: green circuit board shards, copper wires, reels and springs, fingers and bulbs, screws skittering across the concrete floor of an empty garage. Fractions litter the process. When jagged plastic splits skin and blood remainders drip over oil stains, you must subtract and divide again. The big black ants that live in the driveway cracks have three body segments. After you slice with your dad's boxcutter, one thorax remains. Seventeen nail holes punched through the mason jar lid provide enough air for five fireflies. Hurled against concrete, the holes provide nothing. Four fly away and one's body glows ooze across a hand-scoop of glass slivers. You can gather up the glass pieces, the lawn mulching, two orange maple leaves. You can try to measure the difference between a pebble and a rock, but there will always be dirty decimal points trailing into infinity. By sundown, the table saw has decapitated ten G.I. Joes and three Barbies and your mother's two headlights still haven't lit up your driveway. Dad's inside, tapping one graphite nub of a Number 2 pencil against your homework. He's ready to help when you are. He's ready to help you show your work, ready to explain shared custody, every-other-weekends, alternating holidays. But you can't get to a stopping point with a whole integer. Remainders persist: five tennis ball halves, four tiny General Lee tires, one wasp nest, two tire tracks that aren't coming back.

73

THE LIFE NET

Because who else will catch you when you must jump, when there's no other path but plummet? Because when you're quaking from your third-floor window, smoke blackening your vision, flames singeing skin, we are salvation. Because is why we exist. We are the beaming white circle in darkness, the red bullseye. We, the fine firefighters of this great blistering nation, will catch you in our life net. So, jump unto us.

Or, first, watch as we demonstrate the miracle. We swivel from half-moon storage position to locked life-saving circle in seconds. This is how we've rescued for a century, since Thomas F. Browder, our inventor, first rustled from epiphanous dreams to scribble circumferences and springs on the plaster wall beside his bed, since his ingenious patent in 1887. We stow Browder's likeness in lockets against our chests, tap them and pray to our saint of ingenuity, always ask what Browder would do, because Browder knows best. You may be thinking—you up there on the roof with your arms crossed over your chest and your pursed lips and your pissy posture and your cordless phone and your blissfully cruel certainty in our obsolescence—that we are superstitious relics, that we are clowns clinging to a trampoline. It is not a trampoline. We disdain that conflation. We say life net or safety sheet, because we are not children playing with toys. We are men, and one woman, saving lives.

The one being Gertie. Just watch her and us grip the metal frame, huddle shoulder to shoulder, shuffle across the sidewalk in perfect synchronicity. You smirk at our ballet, scoff at the beauty of grace under crushing pressure. You shake your head at our chorus of grunts, and we forgive you your cynicism. Suit yourself spectating from the clocktower of the tallest building around, the four-story town hall. We'll be back for you when you're ready.

Watch: a woman, a mother, shins stretched over the windowsill, sooty tangles flouncing over her eyes. Look more closely at what she proffers in her outstretched hands: a baby, a child, can't be more than one year old, complete innocence. The child does not squirm. Stoic calmness soothes their limp limbs. The child is not dead but curious, as you should be if you'd stop trying to dial an operator from the clocktower and allow yourself admiration and just witness. We are the first and only responders.

The mother's hands part and the child is baptized by floating, freefalling from fire and smoke and collapse. This child turned angel. We raise our arms, hoist the life net's frame. At the instant of impact, the moment bare thighs meet safety sheet, we drop so sweetly, become pillow, feather, perfection together. Then we tilt one side and the infant rolls into Rolland's arms. The child does not cry, is preoccupied plucking at Rolland's fine auburn whiskers.

We forgot the mother, you narrate into your camcorder. You aim the lens at her, zoom in, click the back of your throat, assume we can't handle a third-floor adult. Which would then mean that you, all the way up there, are hopeless. Fear not. Behold. She takes coaxing, and Cecil is our golden boy with big green eyes and perfect teeth, and he convinces her to fly through a series of waving arms and throaty murmurs. Her skirt billows in the air, and we glance only to gauge descent, never to notice the white panties with the tear against the right buttock. We catch and she's safe in Cecil's arms, then reunited with child—a Madonna glowing atop Browder's miraculous arc of saving.

Yes, watch as we don't linger for the crowds to flash their Polaroids and Instamatics. If you won't abandon your electronic marvels and jump now, then we're off. And so we go deeper, where town bleeds into city, where ten-story buildings prick the skyline, where the FM radio towers needle at God. We eye black billows, smoldering roof tar and treated lumber ablaze. Our hearts thrill, yet we won't crack smiles. That would be insensitive. That would be betrayal. We must hate the fire we live to best. We must hurry somberly, the precious lift net folded and hoisted across our shoulders.

The burning culprit stretches high, and we exhale a secret sigh that there are only eight stories to this apartment complex. Any higher and the life net flirts with failure. Flames spout out some windows. Out others, survivors flap yellowed blankets. There are dozens trapped, to which Browder will deliver salvation. We snap open the life net and huddle into position. The low floors first, where we are confident in spring support, in the alloy wire mesh's tensile strength. We catch three children, two men, four mothers, one senior with hair the color of ladder rungs, two cats, two dogs, and one boa constrictor that coils into a question mark around the bullseye. Our biceps and forearms ache with success. Our thighs throb, and Elmer's bad knees are getting worse, but adrenal pride remedies all. We will not be stopped.

One final cry stings the air. An ancient man bellows from the seventh floor, yelling through his naked gums, orange flames reflected in his bare scalp. He may only have a handful of months left, but he shrieks and flails to keep them. With his leopard-print liver spots, he certainly doesn't create a photo opportunity, wouldn't be fit for the newspaper front page that we wouldn't smile for anyway. We don't rescue for fleeting glamour.

We hup-hup-hup in formation to his window and spread the net. We worry about soft bones but you and he and we must remember that all we can offer is a chance, a better option than burning. So we plead for this curmudgeonly hermit to make haste into gravity's grip.

He ducks back inside smoke. After too many scalding seconds pass, he pops his silver beard out the window. His arms hug a stack of books. He rains leather-bound Mellvilles and first-edition Cathers. Their golden typefaces shimmer, but their beauty means nothing to Browder, nothing compared to even a single thread-bare life. We flap their splayed pages onto the sidewalk and shout for him to jump. He's busy, though, pelting the bullseye with copper statues, pewter paperweights, silver medallions.

Then lithographs and lamps and cigar boxes and silk robes and knobby bronze doorknobs hail downward. This exhibit of curios ricochets into our chests and faces. We turn our heads, lose our rhythm, and this must be why we miss the ancient hoarder's jump.

His drop yanks our arms before we understand our catch, and then the storm is over. Nothing stirs. When we finally gather the courage to witness, we see that the man has landed atop his treasure. A bronze cowboy's arm pierces the man's esophagus. His neck whiskers gleam with ruby wetness. His spine zigs over hardbacks and sepia globes. Instead of seizing a final few nonagenarian months, instead of even a few more wheezing breaths of smoke, he has died in our net. The life net's canvas stains with his blood, the red bullseye now blurred into an amorphous oval.

But we don't have time for bleach or grief. There is work to do and we plunge into the city's tentacle streets. A ladder truck rockets past our foot-soldiering. The smoke it chases hasn't even crept into our nostrils, must be miles away, so we stalk the siren's echoes. If there's a chance to lend our hands, callused from the life net's metal frame, then we must persist. Into the sunset we march, trailing the last decibels of siren song.

Once the sun sets, the world seems on fire—one thousand lights spritzing halo-orange glow. Night and day blur behind electricity's bullying. Years could be passing while we wander and wonder at the municipal sprawl, and we are tricked. Elmer tugs the life net right toward a blinking neon-pink Live Nudes sign. Solly pulls left toward the simmering red pawn store promise: We Buy Gold. We lurch toward the fluorescent plastic flames advertising a fast-food flame-broiled burger. The customers gawk over suspended sandwiches while we stare through the window, stomachs growling and faces hot, life net at the ready. Rolland wonders if we better just give in and go home.

Then a glorious blazing appears. It alights the night sky. The city's tallest factory spits fire. Two ladder trucks are already on scene, cranked up through black clouds. We can't see our comrades working up there, through all that smoke, but we assume their greatness, tap our Browder lockets and pray for the best, recite his patent: *combine simplicity, strength, and efficiency, together with capabilities of being packed in a small compass.* We hope their usefulness will exist in perpetuity. Likewise, Browder's legacy must not be forgotten. The jump for one's life must remain an eternal human right.

We've been fumbling through the city for years perhaps, long enough for towers to erupt everywhere. We must admit how our heads dizzy gazing up at untested peaks. We scour the factory building's base, hunt survivors hanging out of low-level windows. They have already evacuated. All that's left are the heights, and it hurts too deeply to admit inability. What choice do we really have? Do we dare depart from danger, from a single life that could be saved? We raise the life net, flash its bullseye and the ancient hermit's dried blood toward a fourteenth-floor man clad in a navy-blue uniform, stitched nametag winking from his heart. He seems unsure, takes something from his pocket, and a blue screen glows. And so we know it is you again, from your rooftop to this new height where you brandish your new gadgets that we don't understand, for which Browder didn't have time to amend his patents. What could you be doing with your pocketable screen instead of taking a chance at saving your life? The longer you tap and swipe and stare and plead into it, the farther the flames. The factory lengthens as we linger at the bottom bolstered by Browder's brave spirit, yet you ignore us for that blue-glow sanctuary.

No more hesitation. Jump foolishly and fully. Release your tech and trust in straightforward mechanics, in simple physics, in one man's design of springs and metal and mesh and machine screws. You finally jump, and, true, we've never practiced a catch from this height, not even with the watermelons Sergio supplies from his garden and then pitches off the roof of town hall. Sergio's eyes flash the terror of uncertainty now, as all our eyes do. Our necks contort up at that smoke-laced sky, at your eternal descent. And we miss. Or you miss. Of course all of us will miss at some point, even those gargantuan ladder trucks. There will never be enough of us to catch all who must jump. And Rolland is struck by falling limbs. He crumples.

We couldn't save you and your future-stuck dawdling, and now we bow around Rolland, check breathing, pulse, administer

CPR, shout to the ladder trucks for whatever electrical marvels they've stashed inside their state-of-the-art metal beasts. But they don't hear us. They're too busy dragging ragdoll bodies down their ladders. There's not enough time, never enough. We kiss Rolland's hands, hug his neck. Another body crashes through the net while only half of us are still holding. This plummeting corpse is a blur ripping through the life net's fabric. We can't bear to examine the tear, the bone-blood slurry beneath our precious circle, can't bear to see Browder's patent shredded.

With clenched fists, we tug the fabric taut. Gertie heaves Rolland over her shoulder, then onto the life net. We carry him away from a city grown too big for nets. We hustle like aimless animals. Our circle of saving is making circles, we realize, as we pass the blazing factory again. Or maybe this is a new fire. Or maybe every building burns.

Bodies tumble and streak and smack around us, aiming for our ruined net and Rolland's body. We dodge dozens. Hundreds. We are unable and ashamed and tuck our chins to whisper apology to Browder's locket likeness. How can any force prepare for the kind of explosion that is the city, the future, the corrupted cataclysm of knowing too much yet still unable to control a fire? Even Browder, that brilliant saint, never could've anticipated.

If we could, we'd raze every building down to six securable floors, maybe four, maybe just single stories too squat to ever pose threat. We'd toss your glowing screens on the fire, stand too closely to watch while our own hair curled.

But not yet. Never yet. We have torn mesh and canvas to mend. We will take up needle and thread, sew like mad men and one mad woman. The work never stops. We will aim to be as excessive as water, as fire. Their spilling is endless, as ours will be. Because around this intersection, or maybe around this corner, we'll find our way out. There will be a cliff, a drop-off edge taller than any glass-skinned, steel-boned behemoth. Together we'll jump that edge, lift Browder's life net above our heads, and float down toward safety.

AMATEUR PALEONTOLOGIST STUMBLES INTO MY FOOT

His apprentice lugs an armful of phalanges through my foot, over the arch to his makeshift table, bones like stars against my blushed tendons. These are clues, code he must decipher. Nose slick with sweat, his bifocals slip, teeter the tip of his dusty nose. But he doesn't correct, let's them dangle, slice bone blur through his vision. None of it matches, attaches, the way he wants it to. He bends, fingertips lacing ligament brambles, until a shard pricks, snapped metatarsal. The apprentice and his fat hands, he thinks, cement grip that choked the future by cracking the past.

I've tried to explain how my foot will never assemble brontosaurus, flap off as pterodactyl. What display could a Smithsonian curator construct of my spurs, that ganglionic cyst, miles trod getting lost in towns I should know? I want recovered creation, too. But he won't listen like his apprentice, whose thick calves lift, red sneakers disappearing into marrow forest, stowing himself in the ankle where he crunches their last granola bar and dreams of Parthenon reconstruction, chisels instead of brushes, lunch with marble masons. The paleontologist doesn't eat, inhales bone meal, thirsts for breakthrough, never sated. He will find no genesis here, only calluses and creaking articulations. My foot uncovered, dissembled, cataloged, and put back together equals my foot. But once inside, obsessed, there's no path out, and your skeletons will stab sharp with every step.

FATHER AT SHIFT END

The mill is making, the transmission tower buzzing out, the factory hatching product. We forget exactly what's rolling off the line. But somewhere in there, through doors, through brick and shadow, they're making what matters. We smell it through our windows, sulfur and chlorine and burning oil and rubbed rubber and coal and ash and then, past five, dozens of meatloaves baking and golden cornbread and Father unbuttons his navy-blue shirt, sucks it all in, lights a cigarette, as he leaves those halls of production. Two blocks to walk, and Father arrives home to us. Couldn't be more convenient, thanks to those great ghosts who stamp signatures on his paychecks and build houses for men like him and families like us and our house is right here, nearly at Father's work's doorstep. Couldn't be more convenient, unless he'd bought the cozy two-story—the same model home as ours—directly across the street from the factory. Father prefers the five-minute walk. It gives him time to smoke and count chimney stacks and think about what he'll make tomorrow, what we'll make for dinner tonight, what this country will make of the great things he just helped make.

BRANDY'S STREETLAMP

Tonight, like every night, we're ready for dates. Ready to jerk or suck or fuck. Except Brandy. Brandy saves fucking for just one customer. Brandy's in love.

Brandy thinks this guy's gonna marry her and fly her to Tahiti where she'll tan her giant new baby belly in a string bikini. She waits for him now. Bought new pleather pumps, cherry red. Looks like she's a ballerina, the way those high-as-a-skyrocket heels shoot her on her toes. She prances a few steps, out under the streetlamp, and we're thinking she looks pretty as the paintings we saw when we all went to the DIA free-museum day last February because it was too cold to fuck, all those dancing girls that are kind of blurry and turn into a swirl of colors up close. All the right colors on Brandy tonight, under the light.

We stay in the shadows, lean against the brick wall of the tire factory like our granddaddies used to do on their smoke breaks, here where they worked all their lives, where they got jobs for their sons—boys who turned into our daddies—and then our daddies got laid off. Our work will outlast any tire factory.

Irene struts out of the shadows, under Brandy's lamp, to ask her for a light, and Brandy says she don't smoke no more, ain't got a flame. She turns her back, covered in that gray hoodie she wears over her new corset. She peers down the street, watching for that Range Rover to crest the hill and take her to stained satin sheets at the honeymoon suite of the Stop & Go-tel.

Oh, here's mine, Irene says. She pulls out her lighter and lights her smoke and blows a cloud at the back of Brandy's bleach-blond wig.

We bet that smoke's killing Brandy. We bet she lied about quitting smoking, and the craving will chase her all night. Irene returns to our shadows, slams her ass against the grime-smeared brick, says, Bitch putting on a real show for that no-show trick.

When ain't it a show? That's what they want, to see us all lined up in a row, wearing our not-quite best. We tear our thigh-highs, yank down a strap, smudge dirt on asses, let a strand of our bangs curl all wonky. Guys like pretending they can rescue us, extend charity. They're all thinking, My dollars could really help her, and maybe she'll use it to buy a fix, but maybe she'll use it on bologna and bread, on an online class, toward first-month's rent on a quiet studio. Truth is, we use those dollars on whatever the fuck we want.

But Brandy, she puts it all toward new shoes, new fancy tangas she orders online, new corset that cost more than a businessman's blazer. She's looking new every day for one man, and one man ain't never enough for any woman. Not anymore. Not since our daddies couldn't find work and their pensions turned to dust and the men who might've been lovers are scanning want-ads for the same fucking job that none of them will get, waiting for the sun to go down, so they can come find us.

And finally Brandy's guy is coming. Headlights bouncing up the hill, one slightly brighter than the other, like Sway's uneven nipples. Little bit of asymmetry never scared off no date. They like the way Sway's tits look. We like them, too, named the smaller one Jed and the bigger one Elvis. Brandy can't quit glancing down at her own tits, chin buried in her cleavage, neck all smushed up, eyes going cross, like she's looking for notes she scribbled in there with eyeliner to cheat her GED. Brandy's hot as shit, but she wastes it all on this one fucker, who's slowing, turning his face through an open window, looking at Brandy, looking at us, and then speeding up, and there go those taillights.

Brandy waddles toward the disappeared headlights and then stops on the edge of her streetlamp, that bright rim of the bubble. On the other side is night, is us, is what's really going on when this job is just another shitty job.

Irene saunters back into the spotlight, and Brandy glowers at her, balls her fists. Irene, though, she plays it cool, wraps an arm around Brandy's shoulder, puts a cigarette in her mouth, flicks a flame. They smoke together and rock in that light, and this shit is too fucking cute. We want to join them, want to be Brandy in love, want to be Irene the mother. But we stay in the shadows, leaning our asses against Granddaddy's shit-outta-luck tire factory.

Then the uneven headlights pop up again, second lap. Irene faces them, raises a middle finger with one hand, lifts her skirt and flashes her pussy with the other. We laugh. Brandy laughs. That Range Rover keeps on coming and does its slow-to-a-crawl-check-out-the-goods move again. Like he hasn't seen the goods a dozen-hundred times, like he hasn't taken Brandy into alleys and hotel rooms just as many times.

He stops, right next to where Brandy stands, Irene hanging over her shoulder. We can see his squinting eyes, his thin goatee and his starched collar wrapped too tight around his barrel no-neck. He sticks out his pinky finger with the awful chunk of fake gold around it. He points at Irene. Irene, not beautiful Brandy wearing her new shoes.

Irene walks up to the window, leans in, her ass aimed at Brandy. And we're waiting to see if she spits in that asshole's face, or pulls out her knife to give him a good scare, or the mace to send the Range Rover swerving into the stop sign on the next block.

Irene gets in. Down the street go the bumping taillights, eying us like some wolf backing into its cave. Irene's lent cigarette dangles between Brandy's fingers, the cherry so close to sending up her hoodie in the prettiest ball of flames. She's watching the street, waiting. Her ash wilts toward the pavement.

We want to hug Brandy, wrap our arms over her shoulder like Irene did. But we know tomorrow Brandy will stand under her same spotlight, and we just hope she won't be wearing those painful fucking pumps.

DOUG DREAMED IN HOURLY WAGES

At the end of a twelve-hour day, you ringed your neck with a Hooters apron, draped it over your painter whites. Your license had been suspended years ago, so I dropped you off in the Hooters parking lot, exhausted, annoyed at you while loving you, because, fuck, who works like that? We'd already primed and painted two split-levels and a ranch, and I was headed home to shower and collapse while you'd be battering wings and hovering over the miasmic fryer bubbles until midnight, until closing and later, after the girls had rolled their silverware and counted their tips and smoked cigarettes down to the butts, flicking them off into the night as if the butts were their customers' tit-drooling eyes, their wing-gnashing snarls. You probably joined the girls for a cigarette, and maybe rolled them a joint, and when they drove off buzzed and bolstered by beautiful you, you returned to scrub the griddle.

Next morning, I picked you up, you and your son. I drove him to third grade while you spit-combed his hair and listened to him rather than spouting fatherly advice, because we were just kids, too, and you must have been so young, too young, a teenager, when your son was born. I wanted to hate you, the inconvenience of you, for losing your goddamn license a few years after you helped make a human, for making me, a decade later, have to cart your ass around in my Ford Ranger, through the snow, the back tires always slipping in the brumal Michigan sludge, but you were smiling with your chin at this boy between us, and I was studying you a decade before I would become a parent, and you'd been a parent all night on your weekend custody while I'd been sleeping off the last twelve-hour day, dreading another Saturday of painting houses.

I drove you, my employee, my friend, my burden, my champion, for a year. It was a time when anyone who could swing a paintbrush could own a business and make a living because this was pre-recession bliss. We swam in the American Dream replicated a thousand times throughout every Michigan suburb. You can still hear the stamp of foundations crashing into creation, floors and boards and walls and wires, the nailers and compressors pounding, the men laughing and smoking, until we'd come in after the carpet layers and touch up the paint one last time. We'd lose all this, so much, too much. At least half of us would never be paid to touch a tool again, and the homeowners and their first homes and their babies and toddlers and kids would fill the U-Haul and wonder how that dream blinked into nothing.

But I never had to see our work marked with foreclosure signs like grave markers. The subdivisions we built out of thin air and time and materials puffed into a ghost town. I escaped, but just before I left, I visited your apartment to apologize and pay you in cash with a bonus and tell you there was no more work after the boss quit, and your pit bull, that unruly mass of muscles, pummeled my lap and licked my face while you commanded it to stop too calmly, always calm, even when I let you go.

Of course, you had a plan to keep working, and you asked me for honest advice: Did I think you had what it took to run your own painting business? And I couldn't even give you that. I preached at you about working on your brush skills, your cut work, and you nodded, but what an asshole I was. I hope you were thinking that. I hope you hated me for thinking I had a painting hand forged in gold and a brain too good for construction. I hope you imagined punching me out and letting your blissful dog hump my leg. I hope you at least imagined hating me before I left you to your other four jobs, because you were so beautiful, Doug, a creature never sleeping, every hour a wage.

NO GOOD FOR DIGGING

A plumber died in the trenches. The red earth caved, clay swallowing his knees with a hungry sucking, topsoil sounding a startled sigh as it cascaded over him. In that first second of his boots sinking, he thought about wet socks. When the ground viced his chest, he imagined the mess he'd make of his laundry room. In that last sight of sun set past five o'clock, soil stinging his nostrils, he calculated how long it would take to dig out the lateral line. He felt the pipe push into his ankle. He knew he'd be the last to touch it for days. And then the sun was gone.

The plumbers screamed. The women living in the subdivision slid their drapes, called 911. Two roofers hot-wired the landscapers' backhoes, punched at the controls, circled the fresh divot too close and clanged buckets. The tradesmen heard the clang, spilled from their half-built houses: three painters, a Spanish-speaking sanding crew, one framer. They scratched at the earth bare-handed, stabbed with hammers and extension poles. They dug like children aiming for China.

The builder arrived later, parked his hatchback, loosened his tie, gripped a clipboard and cell phone.

Ambulances and fire trucks flashed into the cul-de-sac. Shovels were distributed, the backhoes ordered cut so as not to scoop buried scalp. An hour passed before they found the first pale flash of flesh. Floodlights cut through the dusk, poured over the men, who were brown smears of dirt. It was fingers they found first.

One of the plumbers jumped into the hole and grabbed the hand, pulled, grit his teeth, but the earth wouldn't budge. Inside his pocket, the builder squeezed his car keys' sharp teeth.

A lone officer circled the pit with yellow tape, as if mapping buried gas lines. The sky was black before they reached the plumber's ankles. Two sanders buttressed his limp body while the roofers dug out his legs. They plucked his body free. The men dispersed into darkness. Under the floodlights, set into clay, the plumber's boots remained.

Paramedics placed him on the gurney, the white sheet streaked with red earth. The workers circled the ambulance. One of the painters passed out cigarettes, and they all smoked silently. No one offered the builder one. No one had ever seen him smoke.

The workers flicked their butts into the pit then washed the city's shovels under someone's spigot. They lined them against a fire truck. They locked their houses and went home. The builder stayed, stared at his empty clipboard until a fireman snapped off the floodlights then drove away without sirens. The builder climbed into the pit, tugged at the empty boots, but they wouldn't give.

THE LIFE MODEL

cowers behind my right kidney, this red-haired man, fidgeting with the belt of his robe, pulling it tight against his naked belly. My rib cage looms, a prison of bone bars and chalk locks. I urge him— my throttled heart, pulsing spleen—want him to overcome the shame of flesh, as I cannot do. Always only the inside. I spread my ribs, my surging moth-wing lungs. Enter, life model, stand before this class of artists perched on rib rafters chattering like monkeys, pencils gripped, sketch pads white, no hue more starved. I know. I know: What if they laugh? What if they find you disgusting, unfit for art, for charcoal dust and crumpled page? Let my blood warm you, let our temperatures combine, our fears, combine.

He drops his robe, steps from modest brown cotton around his ankles, bearing fire-haloed skin. The artists hush, choke at the beauty of unguarded, raw red. They will never paint landscapes again!—my bone forests and spires alight against striated hills, capillary calligraphy, even this heart that pumps for you. My landmarks cannot compete with your flawed map, freckled skin, curved penis, wrinkles and stretch marks. You are art and I am—body. Body of blood. Body of water and carbon and you, naked and miraculous.

BRUISE ROOM

If you think purple is just a color, then you never spent twelve years caged in white walls. First thing I did after getting early-released from Thumb Correctional was buy a gallon of satin-sheen purple. My sister snuck her name on a lease for my apartment in Detroit. Landlords don't like collecting felon signatures. And I probably wasn't supposed to, probably breaking lease agreement, but rolling that first wall purple was like breathing after a life lived underwater. Purple doesn't care what you did. Purple only wants to blanket you in a big, warm bruise.